HER GUARDIAN ANGEL

When Shelley Rushton discovers that her fiancé, Brent, is milking money from her father's bakery business, she is afraid and runs away. Brent hires a detective agency to track her down, and Sam Gilday volunteers for the job. He eventually finds Shelley living in a remote cottage on the Lancashire moors. Her life is in great danger, and when she confides her fears to Sam he vows to protect her. Then Shelley begins to suspect that Sam is lying to her. What exactly is going on?

*Books by Louise Armstrong
in the Linford Romance Library:*

HOLD ON TO PARADISE
JAPANESE MAGIC
A PICTURE OF HAPPINESS
THE PRICE OF HAPPINESS
CONCRETE PROPOSAL
PATTERN OF LOVE
KINGFISHER DAYS
MASTER OF DIPLOMACY

LOUISE ARMSTRONG

HER GUARDIAN ANGEL

Complete and Unabridged

LINFORD
Leicester

First published in Great Britain in 2001

First Linford Edition
published 2003

British Library CIP Data

Armstrong, Louise
    Her guardian angel.—Large print ed.—
Linford romance library
    1. Love stories
    2. Large type books
    I. Title
    823.9'14 [F]

    ISBN 0–7089–9454–7

Published by
F. A. Thorpe (Publishing)
Anstey, Leicestershire

Set by Words & Graphics Ltd.
Anstey, Leicestershire
Printed and bound in Great Britain by
T. J. International Ltd., Padstow, Cornwall

This book is printed on acid-free paper

1

The woman behind the counter of the petrol station had made no attempt to disguise herself. Sam Gilday slid farther behind a rack of motor oil and double-checked the glossy photograph in his hand. The detective agency had been given a picture of a woman who was beautifully groomed, smiling, wearing an evening gown that displayed her creamy shoulders as she leaned forward in an attractive pose.

The woman behind the counter wore no make-up, her hair was scraped back from her face, and she was wearing a polo shirt embossed with the words, **Tom's Garage — Happy to Help You**! But it was undoubtedly the same woman, Shelley Rushton. He'd found her at last.

The sweet taste of success surged through Sam's veins and he felt exultant. More than once over the last week he'd wondered what on earth he was doing, playing at detective and not even finding the woman, but now the hunt was over. He could ring his old friend, Dwayne, and tell the man to eat his words. Dwayne had openly ridiculed Sam's offer of help when a staffing crisis had left his detective agency in chaos, but with no experience and no training, Sam had cracked the case.

He couldn't wait for Dwayne's reaction when he heard that the missing woman had been found. Sam realised that he was heartily glad the experience was over. It had been interesting, he supposed, and a part of him had enjoyed the chase, but the rôle of detective wasn't for him.

He felt unexpectedly sorry for his quarry as he put the photograph back in his pocket, but that was no surprise. His mission in life was to help people, not to hunt them down. He'd ring Dwayne, officially end his involvement in the case, and then he'd be free to make the most of the few days of holiday that were left to him before he took up his new post.

He could take a long weekend in Paris, or he could visit his sister in Gibraltar and be introduced to his new nephew, or . . . Sam's thoughts trailed away as he realised that the woman behind the counter was looking at him curiously. He'd read enough detective stories to know that he'd been lurking around the garage's twenty-four hour shop long enough to make her suspicious. Better make a move.

Sam picked up a small can of motor oil, and then walked over to the fridge and selected a carton of orange juice for the long drive home. When he got to the counter, the customer in front of him was taking his time about paying for his petrol. The man's aim seemed to be a date with Shelley.

Sam watched her curiously as she fended him off. Short, fair, curved, she wasn't Sam's type, but as he looked rather more closely, he saw that her hair shone and, even under the harsh fluorescent lights, her skin had a soft lustre that made her look natural and healthy. She handled the man skilfully, blocking his advances without hostility or overreacting. She handled her work competently as well, and as Sam paid for his goods, he wondered how she'd learned her way around the garage so quickly.

He knew for a fact that only a week ago she'd been running her family's bakery and sandwich business, a business she clearly took a keen interest in. As he walked away, Sam could hear Shelley quizzing the next customer to step up to the counter about his choice of sandwich. Still, the affair was nothing to do with him, and, from the fact that it had been the fiancé who'd wanted her found, Sam guessed that a lover's tiff had driven her away. Dwayne had told him that the fiancé worked at the company, too, and that could be a claustrophobic situation. He felt unexpectedly sorry for Shelley Rushton as he walked towards the exit.

As the automatic doors opened, a blast of freezing air met Sam. Snow swirled in the darkness. He sprinted for the shelter of his car and turned on the engine to warm up the interior. He took his phone and automatically punched in Dwayne's number. Then Sam remembered that his orders were to contact the fiancé, a man called Brent Dughall, personally.

He was about to redial, when he realised that his mobile phone wasn't working. He looked at it with exasperation. He didn't know if it was the snow storm or the Lancashire hills blocking the signal, but he'd have to go back into the garage and use their public phone.

He pulled his coat over his head and battled against the storm towards the bright neon shop sign. He'd expected the shop to have emptied, but a burly man was using the pay phone and a skinny, very gaudily-dressed woman was waiting behind him. She eyed Sam with predatory interest.

'Has the storm stopped you driving, darling?'

'I'll have to ring my boss about continuing,' Sam answered.

Her smile held an unmistakable invitation.

'I'm just ringing my kids to make sure they've gritted the drive. I don't live very far away if you need a place to spend the night.'

'That's very kind of you,' Sam said, hiding inward revulsion as he took in the avid expression below the frizzy hair. 'But I should be all right in my four-wheel drive.'

The burly man had finished his conversation. He offered the phone to the skinny woman and turned to Sam.

'You'll need more than one of those toy cars to get through this snow. I'm spending the night in the cab of my lorry. Death, those roads are.'

Sam cast a glance at the howling darkness outside the plate glass window and reflected that the man might be right. A true blizzard was blowing up. The skinny woman finished her call and handed the phone to Sam. He dug in his pockets and swore softly! It was a good job he was only a pretend private eye. Now he was going to have to ask Shelley for some change. She gave him her easy smile as she hunted for some coins in her own purse.

'I can't open the till unless there's a transaction,' she explained.

The educated tones of her low, attractive voice reminded Sam that this woman was a princess. He wondered why she'd run away from her kingdom. He met her eyes curiously as she handed him some change. She had well-shaped dark brows and lovely, violet-coloured eyes rimmed with thick lashes. What could have driven her away? Why was she choosing to work the late shift? And where was she living? This garage was situated in the middle of some very lonely moors. It was miles to the nearest town.

Sam played with the coins in his hand as he walked across the now-empty shop to the pay phone. He hesitated before picking up the receiver. What if Shelley overheard his conversation? Then the doors slid open and a slim figure in a duffel coat blew in. Shelley looked at the clock, which showed five to twelve, and spoke to the newcomer.

'I was afraid you wouldn't make it.'

The slim figure shrugged off the soaking wet coat to reveal a rather spotty-faced young man.

'I need the money,' he replied, and Shelley gave him a sympathetic smile.

'It'll all be worth it when you're qualified.'

The student wiped his glasses.

'Keep telling me that. Any news of Moira?'

Shelley's face lit up. Sam was knocked out by the brilliance of her smile.

'She's feeling much better. She'll be back tomorrow.'

The student smiled, and then looked sad.

'I'll miss you. Why don't you ask the boss to give you a permanent job? I'm sure he would.'

Sam watched Shelley curiously, wondering what her answer would be.

'I think I'll go for the bright lights next time.'

The student grinned.

'The moors sure are lonely, especially in this weather. But it'll be quiet tonight. I'm hoping to get at least half of my project done.'

Shelley gave him another of her brilliant smiles as she signed off at the till and pulled on a cream-coloured trench coat.

'Good luck with your studies, professor.'

'Take care on the road,' the lad called after her.

Sam stood by the phone, shuffling the coins in his hand. If he followed Shelley now, he could find out where she was staying and give the client the full picture. Dwayne had told him that runaway women were usually found with a man. Once Sam had reported to the fiancé that Shelley Rushton was found, the client would surely ask where she was and whom she was with. And he was going to be the perfect private detective if he could tell him. Decision made, Sam slipped out into the night.

Shelley felt freezing air on her face as she picked her way across the deep snow that now covered the carpark. She was glad to be driving a solid, four-wheel-drive vehicle. She wouldn't have dared take a lighter car into the howling whiteness that was blowing around her. She started the Range Rover's engine and drove cautiously on to the main road.

Even though both lanes had been gritted, she was surprised to see how many other cars were out so late at night. Where were they all going? Where had the handsome man who'd taken so long to select his motor oil been going?

She wondered if he was married. Probably. He had the face of a man who would have lots of friends and strong relationships. He wouldn't become a workaholic, not like Brent, her fiancé — her ex-fiancé.

Shelley bit her lip and peered over the steering-wheel and out into the wild night. There, she'd said it. The thought had been bubbling around in her mind ever since she'd stormed out of Brent's office, slamming the door on her way. Brent Dughall was no longer the man she wanted to marry. The feeling had been building up in her for months, and it had crystallised into certainty the moment Brent had shouted at her. Shelley finally let herself relive the events that had led to her running away.

Realising that it was more than a month since she and Brent had done anything recreational together, she had slipped up to his office at the end of the working day, meaning to suggest they have dinner at a restaurant that night. The office had been empty. Shelley had idly picked up a pile of delivery notes that lay on his desk when the door banged open, and Brent raced across the room, his face wild with anger.

'What the blazes do you think you're playing at?'

Astonished, Shelley let the delivery notes fall from her fingers.

'Brent, what's the matter?' she asked.

He tried to collect himself then, gathering up the papers with an attempt at a laugh.

'I can explain these notes.'

'Notes?' Shelley asked, staring at him in bewilderment. 'I'd rather you explained why you shouted at me like that.'

Brent folded the delivery notes small and stuffed them in his pocket.

'I don't like people breathing over my shoulder.'

'Brent, you can't be so secretive about company matters. Perhaps I shouldn't have picked them up off your desk, but they're only delivery notes, and I have every right to see them. Why are we ordering so much ordinary flour, by the way?'

Brent's eyes flickered and then opened very wide.

'The flour mill made a mistake. They sent us regular flour instead of organic. I've rung them up about it.'

'We're talking about work again,' Shelley said, feeling sad.

'Don't go all female on me! You know we agreed not to mix work and relationships,' Brent ordered.

'Do you still think we should get married?'

Brent answered at once.

'Of course, I do, darling.'

But he made no move towards her, and Shelley saw nothing in his eyes that could be described as love. She spoke sadly.

'Do you realise that it's more than a month since we did anything together?'

Brent's eyes flickered.

'Then we'll take a recreational break this weekend. Satisfied?'

Shelley looked at his handsome face

and realised that she hardly knew the man he'd become.

'I don't think this relationship is going anywhere, Brett.'

Now she had Brent's full attention.

'What will your father say if we split up?'

Shelley felt her voice tremble as she answered.

'Don't let it affect your work for him and he probably won't even notice!'

Brent took a step towards her and opened his arms.

'Darling! You're getting upset. Let's not quarrel.'

Shelley made no move towards him and regarded him steadily.

'I'm going away for a few days to think about things.'

'You can't rush off in a huff just because we've had a few words.'

'I need space.'

'Do I have to remind you that you hold a responsible position with this company? How am I going to raise the loans for our new expansion if you don't meet with the backers next week?'

Shelley felt tears sting her eyes and her hands shook as she stood regarding the man she had been going to marry. She felt as if a cold stone had landed in her stomach, but she felt a red hot anger, too. Brent's true concerns were clearly revealed. If he ever had cared for her, he no longer needed her now he'd made managing director by his own efforts. He thought of nothing but the company. The realisation had sent her storming out of his office, and set in motion the chain of events that had since led to this wild drive at midnight along a snowbound road.

Shelley left the main road at a crawl and carefully negotiated the slip road. There was much more snow on the smaller roads. She had to circle the roundabout at fifteen miles an hour, and when she reached the unlit road that led to the cottage where she was staying, she was forced to engage the four-wheel-drive and drop her speed to five miles an hour.

She couldn't believe it when she saw headlights behind her. What other clown would be on this road tonight? A shiver of icy suspicion trickled down her spine. Where were they going? The holiday cottages along the lane were empty except for hers. No-one else was fool enough to rent a house on the moors in January. An uneasy, primitive suspicion formed in her stomach and yet who could be following her? Nobody knew she was here.

After storming out on Brent, she'd been driving aimlessly north when she'd stopped for petrol and seen a hand-written notice advertising for temporary staff. She still didn't know why she'd taken the job, unless it was to keep her mind so busy that she wouldn't have to think about her problems with Brent, and her father.

All right, it hadn't been the brightest of ideas to lose her temper so thoroughly, but to have her own father take Brent's side over her own had left a bad taste in her mouth. But whatever the provocation, she'd said more than she should have done, and when she'd rung home in case he was worrying, her father's cool tones had made it clear that she wasn't forgiven.

The wheels of the big car she was driving slipped on the packed snow. Shelley reminded herself to keep her mind on the road, and the headlights that flashed in her mirror. The turn-off to her cottage was only a quarter of a mile away. What if someone was following her? She'd be a fool to lead them right to her house.

Shelley's knees shook and it was hard to keep her feet steady on the pedals. This lane was too narrow to turn and go back to the main road, and once she turned into the side road the cottages were on, she was committed to going home. The road petered out into moorland a few yards beyond the last building. Shelley looked in her mirror again. The lights were still there. She had a mobile phone in her handbag, but whom could she ring? Not Brent, that was for sure. She'd rather face a madman than phone her fiancé and say she needed his help. And not her father. He was supposed to be looking after himself since his last angina attack. She couldn't ask him to turn out in this weather.

The windscreen wipers swept monotonously across the windscreen in front of her. It was so dark out there, and the whirling snowflakes made hypnotic patterns that made it difficult to think. Then Shelley had a brainwave.

'Farmer Hawthorne!' she said aloud.

Halfway down the steep, bendy road was the farm where she'd rented her cottage. Shelley made a sharp right into the farm gateway and drove into the yard. She felt like a fool as the other set of car lights carried steadily past her and down the road. No-one had been following her at all. It was her overheated imagination.

She sat quietly in the big car, feeling her heartbeat slow down and her frightened breathing return to normal.

She was glad that no-one came out of the farmhouse to investigate. It might be true that a wasted precaution was better than a disaster, but she'd rather not have witnesses to how stupidly nervy she'd been.

Shelley put the big car into gear and drove back on to the main road. She was only ten yards from the turning that led to her rented cottage when she saw the headlights returning. As the white beams swept around the bend in the road she was caught in the glare. Terror washed over her and all her primitive fears returned.

He had been following her and now he was back. She was trapped. In a frenzy of fear she jammed her foot down hard on the accelerator and tried to race past the other vehicle. But she'd underestimated the effect of the icy surface and the narrowness of the lane. She heard metal screeching on metal as the solid body of her Range Rover banged into the other vehicle, and then none of the pedals was responding, and she was sailing through the dark night for all the world as if she were flying an aeroplane rather than driving a car. Then the front of her vehicle hit the solid stone walls that ran along each side of the moorland road.

She was dizzily aware of the impact spinning the car around so fast that the back end of the vehicle slammed into the wall. But then the steering-wheel came up to meet her forehead and her awareness of the world cut out like a screen going black.

2

Sam had felt exultant when the Range Rover turned into the farm gateway. He drove until he was out of sight around the next bend, then slowed his car to a halt. He took a torch from the dashboard and opened the large-scale map that lay next to him. It was easy to locate the farm, and apart from three cottages a few yards away on the sweetly-named Pippin Lane, there was no other building for miles.

He scribbled down the farm's address in his notebook and folded the map, smiling. He'd go back to the garage, ask who owned the farm, and then he'd have all the information his client needed. He put the car into gear and inched along the road until he found a spot wide enough to turn.

He was beginning to think that he would have made a great detective. He was humming to himself as he retraced his path to the main road. And then he drove around the bend and headlights blinded him. The dark, heavy bulk of the Range Rover was on top of him, its weight sending his car flying across the road.

He felt the world lurch as the back wheels of his Jeep slid into a ditch. He didn't know how deep the ditch might be, or if there was water at the bottom. He didn't wait to find out. He opened the driver's door and threw himself out, landing heavily in the thick snow at the side of the road.

His vehicle lurched and then settled a few more inches, its headlights sending crazily-angled beams up into the night sky, illuminating the whirling snow. The engine raced and then went dead. Sam could hear ringing in his ears as he got groggily to his feet. The snow was cold on his exposed skin and blasts of icy wind snatched at his breath. Dread clutched at his stomach. Where was Shelley?

He could hear only the sounds of the storm around him, but he could see the dark bulk of the Range Rover a surprisingly long way down the road. The impact must have propelled her an incredible distance. His heart beat very fast with panic, and guilt. This accident was his fault. Shelley had been frightened by his clumsy attempts to follow her. If she was hurt she'd carry the blame for ever.

Feet slipping on the deep, drifting snow, he raced towards her vehicle. Both the front and the rear end were crumpled. She must have hit the wall with terrific force. The windscreen had shattered. The engine was silent, but the headlights still glared across the empty moorland. The cab of the vehicle was dark and looked empty.

Sam reached into his pocket for his torch. Thank goodness the impact hadn't smashed it. The brilliant thread of light caught the pale shape of Shelley's face. She lay slumped over the steering-wheel, her arms dangling as if she were asleep. Her eyes were closed. Sam's stomach lurched. A trickle of blood glistened crimson against her pale skin. He pressed his finger to the satiny smoothness of her skin at her throat. He felt the flutter of her pulse. He knew that people who seemed to be unconscious could often hear sounds from the world about them.

'Shelley, my name's Sam. I'm a doctor. I'm going to examine you to see if there are any bones broken.'

He was aware of the wind howling above him as he examined her quickly. Hope grew with every passing second. The only injury he could find was the knock she'd given herself on the steering-wheel. He brushed the hair back from her pale forehead and examined that area more closely. The bleeding had already stopped and his trained fingers could find no evidence of serious damage.

She moaned slightly and shifted her position. Sam lifted her lids and examined her eyes. She was still unconscious. He stood back and regarded her thoughtfully. It went against all his medical training to move her, but if they stayed out here, she'd freeze.

He sprinted back to his car and retrieved his mobile phone. There was still no signal. He hated the feeling of being cut off. Yes, he was a doctor, and the Navy had trained him to be self-sufficient, but what wouldn't he give for some medical back up now?

Knowing it was vital to stay calm, Sam tried to think of Shelley as a training exercise, but he couldn't dismiss a sense of personal responsibility for her that was growing by the second. He forced himself to walk back to her slowly. It wouldn't help either of them if he slipped and broke a leg. His legs tingled with the cold wetness of snow, but he knew they'd soon be numb. He had to find shelter, and fast.

When he got back to the Range Rover, Shelley was still unconscious. He wouldn't move her until he'd decided where to go. He saw a handbag, lying open in the footwell with the contents spilling on the floor. He reached for her mobile phone, hoping for a signal, but although she used a different network, it, too, was dead. Then he saw the label on the keys that lay half out of her handbag — Hawthorne's Holiday Cottages, No. 3, Pippin Lane.

Sam visualised the map he'd consulted before the accident. The cottages were closer than the farm. Decision made, he reached into the cab of the vehicle and carefully lifted Shelley's unconscious body. He wanted to keep her as still as possible, so rather than using the more practical fireman's lift, he cradled her in his arms and fought his way through the storm towards the turn-off for the cottages.

Snowflakes blasted into his face as he walked, stinging his eyes and making it hard to walk in a straight line. He held the torch gripped between his teeth, but cold air rushed into his open mouth and soon made his teeth ache. He was fit and used to heavy work, but Sam was supremely glad to see the dark row of cottages.

He eased Shelley's weight closer to his chest and fumbled for the key with numb fingers. The door opened easily, and there was a light switch right by the door. Sam entered the house quickly. He revelled in the warmth and the feeling of safety. The front door opened directly into the living-room of the cottage. In front of him stood a couch piled with sheepskins. He walked over to it and tenderly laid Shelley in the middle of the soft white fleeces. Then he stood upright and peeled off his wet coat, swinging his arms vigorously to get some feeling back in them. Then he saw the glowing panel of a burglar alarm by the cottage door. Digital numbers were rapidly counting down towards zero.

'Suffering submarines!' Sam moaned.

He sprinted for the panel and examined it. The last thing he wanted was a bell ringing all night. Surely they'd have a simple alarm system that holidaymakers could use easily. He looked down at the bunch of keys in his hand. There was a sequence of numbers printed on the tag for the front door key. Breathing a quick prayer, Sam punched in the code. To his relief, the numbers stopped counting down. The digital display flashed once and then came up with the message, **Disarmed**. Now he could concentrate on Shelley.

He looked around the cottage. The main room had a big, stone fireplace and an assortment of chintzy furniture. The fire was ready to light, and a box of matches lay on the hearth. Sam stooped down and put a match to the fire before heading for the kitchen. It was a neat, characterless room, but just as he'd hoped, it contained a first-aid kit, and hot water came out of the tap. Sam filled a bowl and went back to Shelley.

The fire crackled as it caught light and the shadows played across her delicate features. Sam took one elegant wrist in his hand and stood looking down at her as he took his patient's pulse. She was prettier than he'd thought at first. The soft light showed off her bone structure. She had a straight, perfect nose and a strong, almost defiant chin.

Sam brushed a few wisps of hair from her forehead and gently bathed the broken skin. The cut had stopped bleeding and he could see it was nothing. He smoothed on antiseptic cream and then stood back, thinking. That feeling of being alone and far from help still gnawed at him, but there was no phone in the cottage and Shelley wasn't sick enough to risk carrying her through the storm. So far as he could tell, she had nothing but a mild concussion. The best thing for her now was rest.

The cottage stairs were steep and narrow, but Sam decided that the benefits of a comfortable bed out-weighed the problems of moving her. This time when he lifted Shelley in his arms he became aware of warmth and a faint trace of perfume. His reaction surprised him. Where was his impersonal medical mask? Sam turned into the bedroom and laid Shelley carefully on the bed. He must feel unsettled because he was responsible for the accident. He took a deep breath and called on all the discipline of his training. He'd need it. Her clothes were unpleasantly cold and soggy with melting snow. There was nothing else for it — he'd have to undress her.

He started with her shoes first, unlacing them and putting them under the radiator to dry. Then he peeled the wet socks from her perfectly-shaped feet. Next he took off the white trench-coat and then he stopped and looked at her polo shirt. He reached out and took a handful of material. It was wet through. He didn't want to move Shelley too much by pulling the shirt over her head, so he walked down to the kitchen and rummaged until he found a large pair of scissors.

Back in the bedroom, he took several

steadying breaths and summoned up all his professional detachment before slicing into the fabric. It was hard to stay calm as he gently drew aside the scraps of wet cloth, revealing the black lace flowers of her bra lying against her pale, almost luminous skin. He could see her body moving with each gentle breath.

His own breath caught in his throat as he reached for the button of her jeans. He put his arms under her waist, lifted her and then slipped the wet denim down her bare legs. Her underwear would dry quickly, Sam decided, and he truly couldn't take off any more. He shook out the quilt and then tucked the covers over his patient.

He took her pulse once more, and then nodded, feeling partially satisfied. His medical training told him that she'd be fine, but his primitive self was on full alert, jangling with the need to protect the helpless female who was now in his care.

The next morning, Shelley drifted to

the surface of consciousness, aware that a familiar voice was calling her. She rolled on to her side and snuggled deeper into the pillow. It was too early to get up.

'Shelley, wake up now. Shelley, that's a good girl.'

The voice was calm and held authority, but she struggled to place it. She felt as if she knew it, but it wasn't her father or anyone she knew. Then she felt a firm hand on her shoulder, commanding her attention.

'Shelley, wake up!'

Part of her wanted to stay in the cotton wool clouds of sleep, but the voice would not be denied. Her eyes flickered partly open. A magical white light filled the room. She could see snow on the outside sill of the cottage window. A fire crackled in the tiny bedroom grate. Of course — she was in the holiday cottage, the one she'd rented alone. So who was the man? He must have read her mind. Her question was answered by a deep voice.

'My name is Sam Gilday. I'm a doctor.'

Shelley's eyes opened fully and she was gazing at a big, tanned, healthy-looking, dark-haired man. He was wearing a chunky, knitted sweater over his casual dark jeans. He smiled, showing white teeth and two dimples, and held out his brown hand.

Shelley took it cautiously, and then was surprised by how familiar and comfortable his touch was. She looked up at his eyes. They were the colour of polished mahogany, and they were smiling at her.

'Stick out your tongue,' he ordered gently.

Shelley hesitated. She didn't want to look childish, not in front of such a good-looking man, but his air of command never wavered. Reluctantly, she opened her lips and stuck out the tip of her tongue. He examined it intently, and then smiled.

'Nice and pink.'

Now she remembered where she'd

seen his handsome face before.

'You were in the garage last night.'

'You remember last night? That's good.'

Shelley lifted a hand to a sore area on her forehead. She remembered fear, lights scaring her, hot suspicion and pain in the darkness.

'You were following me,' she exclaimed.

Sam looked down at the old-fashioned carpet patterned with roses.

'I hate to admit this, but I took a wrong turning.'

Shelley felt sharp disappointment as she remembered how her fiancé would drive out of his way for miles rather than stop and ask for directions. Were all men the same? Sam was still explaining.

'I didn't know you were you at the time, if you see what I mean. But I thought the road must go somewhere if there was another car on it, so I followed you, hoping you would lead me to where I wanted to be.'

Shelley supposed that he looked so uncomfortable because he didn't like admitting to having been lost. She scanned his tanned face and chastened expression. He was too handsome to be telling her lies. Her stupid paranoia had led to an accident that could have killed them both.

She stirred under the bedclothes, and then pulled up the quilt as she realised she was dressed in nothing but lacy black lingerie. Then she experienced a hot flush of embarrassment as she realised who must have undressed her. She wasn't afraid, just puzzled. She looked up at Sam.

'Where did we crash? How did we get there? And how did you know where I lived?'

'We collided a few yards from the turning to Pippin Lane, and you were carrying a key with an address pinned on the tag.'

Shelley realised what Sam didn't tell her. He must have carried her to the cottage, and she was no lightweight.

She regarded his broad shoulders and strong arms with new appreciation.

'I guess I have to thank you for a lot.'

Sam's body language showed his embarrassment.

'Now you're awake, I'll put on the kettle. Do you prefer tea or coffee?'

He raced down the steep cottage stairs as if he couldn't wait to get away. Not a man who accepts compliments easily, Shelley thought, turning over in bed. Then she saw the chair by the side of the bed. A pillow lay on the floor in front of it and a spare blanket was thrown over one arm. Tendrils of warmth twined around her heart. He must have sat vigil all night, watching over her like a guardian angel.

Down in the kitchen, Sam tugged angrily at the corner of a foil coffee packet. It tore open in the wrong place, sending a shower of fragrant dark powder over his trembling hands and the clean surfaces of the kitchen. He regarded the mess with a kind of baffled fury. What was wrong with him, for goodness' sake? Doctors didn't dissolve into jelly when confronted by a beautiful woman. They stayed calm and in control of the situation.

It wasn't as though he was inexperienced. Sam liked women, and even in the man's world of the Navy he'd always had some kind of a relationship on the go. None serious, he admitted now. He prided himself on his emotional control. Yet now he was gibbering like a teenager over a woman who wasn't even his type, or hadn't been until he'd realised how beautiful she was. A hot swell coursed over him but he concentrated on making the coffee.

Once he had the machine going he stalked into the living-room and reached for the mobile phones that lay on the table. If even one of them had a signal, he'd phone in Shelley's whereabouts and be out of this mess before the situation scrambled his brains completely. Just as he picked up the first phone, he heard a movement behind him and then a voice.

'Hello?'

Sam whirled guiltily. Shelley stood at the foot of the stairs, smiling at him curiously. She was wrapped in an oversized white robe. Sam could hear himself gabbling nervously.

'Shelley! I was just trying to see if I could get a signal on the phone here. You'll be wanting to ring your father, I expect.'

Shelley's beautiful lashes swept open in suspicion.

'Do you know my father?'

'Oh, gosh, no! But everyone has parents, don't they? One mother and one father, usually, and I expected that you'd have one of each and that you'd want to talk to one of them.'

Shelley was eyeing him warily, and no wonder, he thought. He didn't think he'd made such an idiot of himself since the day his voice broke!

Shelley's lips parted and she said in her soft voice, 'Doctor Gilday . . . '

The sound of his name on her lips sent a wave of heat down Sam's spine.

He lifted his gaze to meet the shimmering softness of her eyes.

'Please, call me Sam.'

She was so warm, so vital and alive. It was inconceivable that his stupidity had come close to killing her last night. Sam ached with the sudden longing for his play-acting to be over, but even as he watched Shelley's face, wondering if she'd agree to date him once this farce was done with, the delicate pink drained out of her cheeks and she crumpled softly towards the floor.

Shelley had been about to ask Dr Sam Gilday why the simple act of being caught with a phone in his hand had made him look like a child caught raiding the cookie jar when she felt a cold blackness spreading out from her stomach. She was vaguely aware of her knees folding up beneath her, but before she could hit the floor, strong arms caught her around the waist. She collapsed forward and burrowed into the softness of Sam's warm sweater, but she was aware of the power of the muscles below. This was a man who would never let her fall.

'I'm all right now,' she said, feeling the blackness recede.

Sam held her steady, one hand supporting her waist. He lifted her chin with the other hand, so that he could examine her face. Shelley remembered he was a doctor as she met the warm concern in his brown eyes.

'I'd like you to have an X-ray this morning,' he said.

'It was just a dizzy spell. I'm fine now.'

His gaze seemed to examine her very soul.

'One can never be too sure with head injuries.'

Shelley was aware of the magnetic charm that lay beneath the professional surface — too aware. She reached for the white towelling of her bathrobe and drew the fabric closed across the base of her throat. She felt an electric warmth spreading over her as Sam continued to examine her. He must have sensed her tension.

'My patients usually get a lollipop at this stage.'

Shelley couldn't help laughing out loud.

'Are you a children's doctor?'

She felt strong fingers inspecting the gash on her forehead. She realised that she'd expected his handling of her to be rough, but for all his size and masculinity, his sure touch was as soft as a snowflake.

'I'm taking up a post at a children's hospital next week.'

Shelley tried to relax and keep her voice steady. Why was it difficult to be so close to this man? She'd been to the doctor's before, she reminded herself, and she'd never reacted like this physically. She'd never reacted like this, full stop, not even with her fiancé. All the more reason not to marry Brent, her heart told her firmly, and at last she knew her own mind. No matter how much pressure her father and Brent brought to bear on her, the wedding would have to be cancelled. She looked up at Sam.

'Thank you, Doctor Gilday.'

He had a fleeting impression that Shelley was thanking him for more than tending to her wound, but as he registered the soft pinkness of her lips as they parted and lingered over the soft syllables of his name, he was distracted by the urge to kiss her. He let go of her at once and turned towards the kitchen, calling back over his shoulder, 'Could you manage some toast?'

When he came back into the front room, Shelley was sitting on the sheepskin-covered couch with her feet tucked under her. She looked at him curiously.

'Won't anyone be worried about you? Where were you making for last night?'

Sam had worked out a beautiful story, but face to face with Shelley's enquiring violet eyes, it had deserted him completely. Rather than sound incoherent, he turned the tables.

'And I'm wondering what your story is.'

Shelley circled her arms around her knees and hugged them to her. She looked up at Sam. There was a glimmer of laughter in her extraordinary violet eyes.

'It starts with me waking up to find a strange man in my bedroom.'

Sam couldn't help smiling in return, but he actually knew how much she was hiding, and the knowledge made him feel uncomfortable. He resolved to stop teasing her.

'I'll be a lot happier when you've been examined at a hospital.'

Shelley crunched her toast with enjoyment.

'I'm fine.'

'I'm going to see if I can get a vehicle running,' Sam said, but as he headed for his coat he heard an engine approaching outside.

He opened the front door on to a bright white day. The snowy air was fresh and cold on his cheeks as he looked out. A stocky man in a padded jacket was climbing off a bright red mini-tractor. He stumped down the snowy path, glaring suspiciously at Sam.

'Where's Shelley?'

Sam heard Shelley calling from inside.

'I'm here, Mr Hawthorne.'

Sam followed the farmer inside the cottage. Shelley was standing by the sofa, holding on to the high back for support. Her cheeks were so white that Sam crossed the room in a rush, afraid that she'd collapse again.

'You got up too quickly,' he told her.

Mr Hawthorne bristled like a jealous dog as he watched Sam take Shelley's arm and help her back on to the sofa.

'She needs a doctor,' the farmer stated coldly.

Sam met the farmer's hostile eyes and smiled at the older man.

'I couldn't agree with you more. I'd like her to have a couple of X-rays. Do you think you could help us with transport?'

'I suppose that's your Jeep my men are pulling out of the ditch.'

Sam nodded gratefully. Shelley cut across his thanks.

'There's no way I'm going to Manchester for an X-ray.'

Mr Hawthorne smiled for the first time.

'You don't have to, lass. The student you call the professor rang up and asked me to check on you this morning, and he mentioned that they've opened a temporary clinic in the village hall. There's been a lot of broken limbs with this weather we're having.'

Sam reflected that he shouldn't be so surprised that the local people cared about Shelley's welfare after knowing her for only a week. He hadn't spent a day with her yet, and already his main purpose in life was her well-being. He looked at the farmer.

'If we can get my Jeep going, I'll drive her to the village,' he said.

Mr Hawthorne examined him for a long, silent moment before replying.

'Aye, I'll leave her in your care. I've sheep to feed yet, and all the milking to see to.'

Sam pulled on his coat and retrieved his rubber boots from under the radiator.

'Shelley, can you be dressed by the time I get back?'

She drew together her brows and gave him a defiant look.

'I haven't said I want an X-ray.'

'Doctor's orders!' Sam replied.

He grinned at the indignation in her expression as he followed the farmer back down the snowy path, but it was for her own good. Shelley might be used to giving commands and running a large bakery firm, but Sam would never allow his medical judgements to be overridden. He wondered about the fiancé. Did he let Shelley boss him around? And what had their disagreement been about? The man must have been desperate to have hired a detective agency, still would be desperate because Sam hadn't yet managed to let Brent Dughall know that his fiancée had been found.

Sam was suddenly filled with repugnance, and suspicion. For the first time, he remembered that Dughall had told the agency he was worried about Shelley's safety. Sam was unable to reconcile the vital, glowing Shelley he knew with the description that the fiancé had given of a weak and unstable female who was liable to do something stupid if she wasn't found.

The farmhands got his Jeep going almost at once, but Sam was in a thoughtful mood as he returned to the cottage for Shelley. He'd give a great deal to know what Brent Dughall's motivation might be in giving the wrong impression of his fiancée. Certainly as far as Sam could see. Shelley seemed to be completely in control.

★ ★ ★

Brent Dughall was in a foul mood as he returned to the bar table holding two more glasses of whisky. What a filthy, low-down dive this pub was. The wild-eyed man at his table reached for the glass with a shaking hand.

Brent sat down and looked at the man's pallid face and greasy hair in disgust.

'Are you sure you're up to the job?'

'No worries, man.'

'You're sweating.'

'Give me a deposit and I can get what I need with it. I'll be right as rain after that.'

'I haven't decided to hire you yet.'

The junkie's thin face creased into what might have been a smile.

'Officially, no-one ain't hiring no-one.'

The down-and-out's caution reassured Brent. Maybe the scraggly hippie knew what he was talking about. He handed over a wad of bank notes.

'Hurry up. I don't want to spend more time in this place than I have to.'

As he waited for the junkie to come

back, Brent perched on the edge of the squalid pub chair and moodily sipped his whisky. The place was nearly empty, but if anyone looked his way he pretended to be absorbed in the football match that was showing on the large television screen over the bar.

He hated having to spend time in such a dirty hole, but it had been forced on him. He was in too far to back out now. If he confessed, it would mean prison for certain, whereas if he played his cards right, he may yet carry off his plan.

Brent fell into his favourite day-dream, the one where his personal yacht was cruising over the blue Caribbean waters as he airily explained to his admiring, all-female crew that going to the office every day was for suckers. He was close, so close now, to achieving his dream. If only Shelley hadn't gone snooping into his affairs.

How long would it be before she called in the police? He had to get to her first. A tiny voice in his head asked him if he was sure that Shelley would understand what she'd seen. Shutting her up was a pretty drastic measure.

'I have no choice,' he told the nagging voice of his conscience. 'I can't take any chances. She could ruin all my plans. And anyway, it's her own fault for poking her nose in.'

He reached for his mobile phone. His call was answered quickly.

'Dwayne York's Detective Agency. How may I help you?'

'It's Brent Dughall. Any trace of my fiancée yet?'

'No, Mr Dughall, I'm sorry. There's no report back as yet, but I can assure you that immediately you reported the trace from the telephone call Ms Long made to her father, our operative set off to find her.'

Brent blessed his luck.

'I don't want you to look for her any more.'

'I doubt if any other agency would be able to find Shelley any faster. Have you seen the weather conditions out there?'

'I'm entirely satisfied with your agency. It's more that I've decided that I was over-acting. Now that Shelley has spoken to her father, I'm no longer worried about her safety. She'll come home when she's good and ready.'

'You have a very sensible attitude, Mr Dughall. In our experience, most cases end up that way.'

'Thanks for all your help. Do I owe you anything?'

'The deposit you left should more than cover the expenses so far. We'll contact you if there's any discrepancy.'

'Don't bother if it's a few quid over. I feel as if I've messed you around.'

Brent heard an easy chuckle at the other end of the line.

'Any time, Mr Dughall. It's been a pleasure doing business with you.'

Brent was too cautious to drink any more alcohol, but by the time the junkie returned, he'd bitten his finger-nails down to the quick. The man looked much more alert and spoke crisply.

'Give me the low-down on this detective's Jeep.'

Brent handed over the paper bearing the details.

'And you say the chick's call was traced to Appleton Moors in Lancashire?'

'That's right.'

'Didn't you put no electronic bug in the Jeep?'

'It never occurred to me.'

The lout flashed a gap-toothed grin.

'I'll find the Jeep through the registration number. I've got friends in the police computer centre, I have. Can I borrow your phone?'

Brent felt pleased with his own cleverness. He took a plastic shopping bag from under the pub table.

'I bought us both new pay-as-you-go mobiles. That way we can stay in touch. I paid cash and registered them with false names and addresses.'

'Don't go bugging me with calls every two minutes,' the youth warned. 'Got a photo of the chick? We don't want no mistakes now.'

Brent noticed that his hand was trembling slightly as he handed over a photograph that showed Shelley smiling under some trees on a windy day. The young rogue glanced at it and shoved it in his pocket.

'Give me the money,' he growled.

Brent felt as if he was moving in slow motion, but he picked up his calf-hide briefcase, opened it and handed over a zipped plastic washbag. He heard a metallic whiz as the junkie opened the zip of the washbag, then a shuffling as the greasy fingers counted the banknotes that filled it. Brent was surprised to find that he had no urge to stop the deal.

'I pay you half now and half later. That was the agreement, right?'

The hippie stuffed the new phone and the bulging washbag into his filthy rucksack.

'We never had no agreement, man, but I'll ring you when I'm ready for the other half.'

The revolting character drained his glass and left the pub. Brent gave him a few minutes and then walked out into the cold. The carpark where he'd left his sports car was covered in snow.

'What a climate,' Brent muttered as he climbed in. 'The Caribbean, that's where I want to be.'

★   ★   ★

A few minutes after Sam and Shelley set off through the narrow lanes that led to the village of Appleton, Shelley let go of her tense muscles. Sam handled the Jeep with an easy competence that she found very relaxing. It was a crystal clear, sunny day.

She wasn't fooled by the generous laughing lines of his mouth. This was a man who could be extremely stubborn. She wasn't sure how she felt about his masculine determination to look after her. She wasn't used to it, that was for sure. She felt curious about him.

'You never told me where you were

going before the accident.'

Sam cast her a quick glance before returning his eyes to the road.

'Maybe because I didn't know. I've been visiting an old school friend, and I wasn't sure where to go next. I still have a few days' leave.'

Shelley was troubled by the tone she could hear in his voice. Was she being paranoid, or could she detect a lie? Unconsciously, she looked around his Jeep for clues. He travelled light, that was for sure, or maybe it was a hired car. The front seats and the dash were bare and tidy, very unlike her own cluttered vehicle. Then she saw the keychain that swung from the ignition. A round, metal dog tag bore the name of a Royal Navy ship. His story didn't add up.

'I thought you said you were a children's doctor.'

She saw Sam's head move as he looked at her and then at the tell-tale key ring.

'I left the Forces last month. I trained

with the Navy, you see. I'd always wanted to be a doctor, but my parents couldn't afford medical school.'

Shelley couldn't understand why she felt so suspicious.

'You wouldn't get to treat many children in the Navy.'

'You would if the government sent humanitarian aid to Africa.'

Shelley remembered a recent public appeal. She had sent a collection around the bakery, and matched the employees' contributions with an equal sum of her own money, but Sam had given so much more. She felt ashamed of herself for doubting him.

'I guess the experience changed you.'

Sam laughed lightly.

'You could say that. I applied for my release and then did a specialised course in the States. I was lucky enough to be offered a position at a top children's hospital in Manchester.'

It wasn't luck at all, Shelley thought, looking at his strong, handsome face. It was ability and preparation, but she remembered his dislike of compliments and said nothing until they turned into the village.

'The garage is open. Can we ask them about repairing my car?'

Sam drove straight past the ramshackle building with its one petrol pump and pile of tractor-sized tyres.

'I'll take you after you've been X-rayed.'

Shelley could see from the stern set to his mouth that she was wasting her time, but she felt compelled to protest.

'But you'll want to get on with your holiday, especially if you've only a few days left.'

'After I've made sure you're OK.'

'I'm not your responsibility.'

Sam drove around the village green and pulled up outside the stone-built hall. He turned off the engine and his voice sounded serious in the suddenly quiet car.

'The accident has entangled our lifelines.'

'Superstitious bosh!' Shelley cried aloud.

'Can't you feel it?'

Rather than admit that she knew exactly what he was talking about, Shelley jumped out of the Jeep and slammed the door. She felt the fresh coldness of the moorland air on her cheeks and her feet sank into the deep snow. Sam came around the Jeep and put a supportive arm around her waist. She felt secure inside his arms, but his nearness also aroused her senses in a way she found difficult to cope with.

'I can walk alone,' Shelley cried, trying to pull away.

Sam wouldn't allow her to leave his grasp.

'You nearly fainted earlier,' he reminded her, and he frog-marched her towards the temporary clinic.

A middle-aged lady met them by the door.

'More customers, Doctor Choudry,' she trilled.

The doctor came out smiling. He chatted away as he ushered Sam and Shelley around a set of screens.

'The Woman's Institute battled very hard to arrange this wonderful emergency village clinic. We were a little afraid that no-one would use it, but as you can see, we have had many customers this morning. It is most satisfactory. Please take a seat. Now, what can I do for you?'

Shelley let Sam tell the story. Dr Choudry nodded at the end of the tale.

'You are a medical man also? Yes, I thought so.'

He took an eye-torch from his pocket and turned his kind dark eyes towards Shelley.

'Look to the left, please. It's no good having a medical man in the family, you know. They worry too much. My wife won't let me treat the children if they are ill. She says I am fussing. I expect your fiancé is the same. Look down, please, and up. Good. I see no

59

problems, but we'll take a quick picture to be on the safe side. There is no possibility that you are pregnant?'

The doctor's mistake was natural. Shelley clenched her left hand into a fist and put her right hand over it, although it was too late to hide the engagement ring that shone on her third finger. She felt her cheeks burning with embarrassment.

It was all she could do to mutter, 'I'm not pregnant.'

She continued to feel flustered while they waited for the X-ray to be developed. Sam's concern for her was so obviously genuine that it was no wonder people thought they were a couple. No-one would believe they'd only known each other a few hours.

Dr Choudry came back smiling with the X-rays.

'Lovely and clear,' he pronounced. 'Do you wish to inspect them, Doctor Gilday?'

Sam hesitated and then said, 'If you don't mind.'

Shelley glanced at the baffling black and white negatives that seemed to mean so much to the two men. She could make out nothing but the outline of her skull and her teeth.

'I don't think I like you looking inside my head,' she told Sam.

Dr Choudry smiled and spoke genially to Sam.

'It is very good to know that there is no damage to the skull. Everything should be fine from now on, but don't let her be alone for the next few days, and contact me immediately if there are any problems.'

'I'll keep a close eye on her,' Sam promised.

Shelley bit back her words until they were descending the stone steps of the hall. Her breath puffed out as she spoke.

'You don't have to stay with me.'

Sam looked down at her with his soft brown eyes and said reasonably, 'Someone has to.'

'But not you. I'll ring my fiancé.

He'll look after me.'

Sam stopped and turned his face towards her. Shelley saw the shift in expression behind his steady gaze. He knew she was lying. Her stomach muscles went tight as she waited for him to challenge her. His brows came down in a scowl over his perceptive brown eyes and his mouth tightened, but his words were mild.

'I'll stay with you until he arrives.'

He slipped his arm around her waist and they proceeded to crunch over the snow to the village garage.

Shelley's feelings were in chaos. How come Sam didn't need an X-ray machine to penetrate the personal secrets that were locked up inside her head? And why did she experience a sudden heady rush every time his arm went around her? She might have been tempted to think she was having another dizzy spell if she hadn't been given a clean bill of health only a few seconds ago, and under her confusion was a delicious awareness of being protected, cared for and cherished.

Dr Sam Gilday was a type of man she'd never met before, and she still knew nothing about him. But she liked him. She liked him far too much.

3

Sam opened the oven door and inhaled the tasty aroma of roasting meat. His mouth watered as he popped in a tray of par-boiled potatoes for a final crisping. It had been a long time since he'd eaten an English roast beef dinner, or cooked one, for that matter. He hoped he hadn't lost his touch because he wanted the food to be flawless for Shelley's sake.

Maybe she'd forgive him if he presented her with the perfect meal. He opened the kitchen door and looked up the snowy hillside. He could see Shelley's distant figure trudging through the snow. She'd stuck to her promise to keep within sight of the cottage, but she must have walked ten miles up and down the hill by now. Sam wanted to kick himself. If only he hadn't snooped.

When they got back from the village, Sam had made a light omelette and persuaded Shelley to lie down for an hour after lunch. Alone in the quiet living-room, he hadn't been able to resist a quick look at the heaped pile of papers that lay on the polished table. He'd been hoping to find a clue as to why she'd run away from her family and her fiancé, but so far as he could see, the papers on the desk seemed to be connected with organic sandwiches.

At first he thought he was looking at the results of a professional survey, then he realised that Shelley had done her own market research. She must have asked every single customer that came into the garage what bakery products they bought, and why. He glanced at the laptop computer that sat on the desk and guessed that she had been collecting the results electronically.

'Switch it on if you want to see more.'

'Shelley!' he had exclaimed.

The hurt and suspicion in her violet

eyes was more than he could bear. Why had he played at detective? Sam stood silently wrestling with his conflicting loyalties. He wasn't a real private eye, but Dwayne had employed him in good faith. How much loyalty did he owe his friend? He would have said one hundred per cent, until he'd met Shelley.

He longed to explain why he'd been looking through her personal papers, but what on earth could he say? He looked at Shelley's beautiful face and willed her not to despise him. Her eyes wouldn't meet his.

'I'm going outside to get some fresh air,' she said coldly.

Despite her attempt to be casual, her voice was tight with unspoken betrayal and suspicion. Sam longed to go with her, but he could tell that she needed to be alone.

'I'll get on with dinner,' he replied.

Sam finished peeling the carrots he'd bought in the village shop and took another look out of the door. She'd have to come in soon. The short winter day was closing in. Through the broken cloud, he could see the sun sinking fast behind the long lines of the moorland hills. The white snow was taking on the magical colours of dusk.

Sam stood at the door, feeling the cold air on his cheeks and watching Shelley. She was facing the wind, watching the sunset. What was she thinking? And why had she run away? As Sam got to know Shelley he was convinced she was no quitter, no weakling. So what terrible thing had forced her away from her life and her family?

Sam closed the door and went back to check on the gravy. It looked fine. He prowled around the cottage, snapping on lights as he went, hoping the glow would attract Shelley home. When he switched on the lamp in her room, he saw that her engagement ring was lying on the bedside table. Sam felt an unholy primitive glee. He wondered if he could persuade Shelley to cast aside the diamond and all it signified for good.

What if he told her his whole story? Would she forgive him? His instincts were urging him to grab her the second she came in and confess before his rational self could stop him, but his logical mind kept reminding him of his prior allegiance to Dwayne and to Dwayne's client.

He'd never felt such divided loyalty. His sense of honour was telling him to ring Dwayne as soon as he could, but his newly-discovered allegiance to Shelley was delighted that a freak of the moorland hills meant that his phone wouldn't work, and Shelley's medical condition meant that he couldn't leave her alone while he drove either to the top of a hill or to a phone box where he could use a land line. He would have to endure the situation as it was. Sam pulled the joint out of the oven and basted it.

Meanwhile, Shelley crested the hill for the eleventh time and stopped to take in a deep lungful of clean, moorland air. There was an icy wetness to it that told her more snow was on the way, and her ears rang with the coldness. Shelley lingered on the hilltop despite the fading light. It was so peaceful out on the empty hills.

Her busy, bustling life at the bakery seemed to lie at the far end of a long telescope. How long had it been since she'd taken any kind of break to get some perspective? Her father never took a holiday, so it seemed natural for her to follow suit, but at the beginning she and Brent had taken time out, hadn't they? She could remember theatre outings and dinner dances, but not much in the way of communication or relaxing.

Brent was so much a part of her business world, that's why she'd accepted his ring. It was understandable that she'd gone with the flow, but why hadn't she noticed that Brent worked every weekend, that his obsession with the company was greater than his interest in her? She curled her bare fingers inside her coat pocket, feeling the unaccustomed nakedness of her ring finger.

The family business soaked up a lot of her energy, it was true, but why had she been content to assume that Brent's growing obsession was in the best interest of the company? Even with the new perspective that distance had given her, she couldn't believe how blind she had been. The evidence was there for anyone to pick up, as her sojourn in the garage had proved. She'd been blind and complacent. It had taken a car smash to shake her awake — a car smash and a special kind of medical attention.

Her toes were cold. Shelley turned and looked down at the valley bottom. She could see yellow squares of light in the windows of the middle cottage, welcoming against the blue night that was fast closing in. She started back at a brisk pace. Sam would be waiting.

Turbulent emotions swirled around inside her when she thought of him. Her feelings had been on a roller-coaster since she'd woken up that morning to his smiling chocolate-brown eyes and his bossy concern for her. He was gorgeous, he attracted her madly, but her intuition told her that there was more to him than he was telling her. She didn't doubt he was a doctor, but why had he been acting like an industrial spy? Tonight, over dinner, she'd quiz him and find out.

Dinner, however, demanded her full attention. She didn't have a word to say until it was over and Sam had washed the last dish. He'd built them a roaring fire, and Shelley sank down in front of the glowing blaze.

'Where did you learn to cook like that?' she asked.

'Mum taught me. Here, why don't we sit on these sheepskins?'

'Good idea,' Shelley agreed, as Sam pulled the soft woolly blankets off the sofa. 'Do you think the fleeces are from

71

Mr Hawthorne's sheep?'

'Probably. People seem to be pretty self-sufficient around here. Mrs Hawthorne made the ginger cordial I bought in the village. Want some?'

Shelley watched Sam's strong hands as he poured the glowing liquid into glasses. It smelled delicious as she took a sip.

'It's beautiful. Are you sure you're not slipping me an alcoholic drink?' she teased.

'Not with your concussion! It's only cordial.'

Sam took off his heavy sweater before settling into the cosiness of the sheepskin throws. He was wearing expensive black ski-wear underneath, perfect for the coldness of the moors. The room was so warm now that she took off her own sweater, glad that she'd worn a flattering top and sprayed on a little perfume. She glanced over at the drawn chintz curtains.

'Do you think it will snow again tonight?'

Sam's lips curved in a breathtaking smile.

'Possibly.'

'I thought sailors were good at weather forecasting.'

He laughed, and the warmth in his eyes drew her like honey. Shelley hardly heard his teasing remarks on the unpredictable vagaries of the English weather, she was too busy watching the firelight playing on his face, masking him with mystery, throwing gold highlights around the dark angles that gave his strong face a delicious edge of excitement.

'I know nothing about you,' she said, breaking the silence.

There was a gleam in Sam's eyes that suggested he agreed they should concentrate on a sensible conversation. Shelley wondered if he had felt the same mystical force that had threatened to overwhelm her. She was falling helplessly under his spell.

Sam's gaze lingered on her mouth in a way that dried her throat, and his voice was low and intimate as he briefly described growing up in a large and loving family.

'Do you see much of your brothers and sisters?'

'They're scattered around the world. Mum and Dad live in Australia with my oldest brother. I'd like to visit them, maybe one Christmas.'

'Christmas in the sun,' Shelley said idly. 'I think I'd like that.'

Sam's laugh held a note of pain.

'You can have too much sun. I can't tell you how much I longed for the grey English weather. I used to dream of the smell of rain and the sounds of English birds in the morning. There was nothing but dust in Africa.'

'Can you talk about it?'

Shelley sat silently as Sam told her of the terrible heat, the searing wind that carried away the crops, and with them all hope for the people. She could see the shadow of remembered pain in his eyes, but she resisted the urge to reach out and touch him, feeling that she might disturb his confidences. It was a part of his life she felt that he'd confide to few, yet he seemed comfortable to share his feelings of unease about the path he'd been on, and his growing urge to do more for the children.

'I don't regret my time in the Navy,' he told her, 'but I knew it was time to move on.'

'Children are the future,' Shelley said softly.

A brilliant smile lit Sam's face, banishing the shadows that had darkened his eyes.

'Now it's your turn. I want to hear the story of your life. How did a woman of your calibre end up working in a twenty-four-hour garage shop?'

Sam had been so open about his own past that Shelley knew she couldn't lie to him. She would repay his emotional honesty in kind, but the silence drew out as she struggled to untangle the chain of events she was mixed up in. Sam gave her an easy grin.

'Start with college,' he advised her.

'What did you train as?'

Shelley laughed out loud at the memory.

'I did nothing as useful as train for a career! I studied art, and it was the best few years of my life, despite my father's fury. He said I was wasting my time and his money.'

Shelley felt Sam's deep interest. He spoke in a voice that was as caressing as a summer breeze.

'Do you feel the time was wasted?'

'No! If nothing else, I met my best friend, Heather. I envy her, you know. She lives alone in a cottage in Wales and paints. She had no responsibilities, no burdens, no family reputation to live up to, no staff to consider. She does what she pleases, all day!'

Sam's body language told her that he was listening intently, but he said nothing to stop the flow of memories. Shelley tried to put her thoughts in order so that she could tell him what her life was like.

'I had to leave college when Dad had

his first heart attack, and I've always been sorry that I never finished my degree. We have a bakery, you see. It's a family business and I'm the only child. My mother died when I was young. Everyone thought my father would marry again, but he turned into a workaholic instead.'

'Is that what you're running away from, the company?'

Shelley's heart beat uncomfortably fast.

'I'm not running away. I'm just having a few days' break. Is there anything wrong with that?'

Sam's gaze was sharp and intent.

'Then you're running away from your fiancé.'

'No, I am not!'

Sam said nothing and Shelley dropped her head to her knees.

'Yes, I am,' she admitted. 'I've been engaged for ten months. Brent Dughall came to work for my father and became his right-hand man. He was the son Dad never had, the golden boy who'd studied law instead of art. He did everything right and was rewarded with my hand in marriage. It's all my fault that we had an accident last night, you know. I panicked because I thought Brent was following me.'

She looked up and saw Sam staring into the fire. There was a stillness about him and a tension. She tilted her head, puzzled by the odd expression on his face.

'Are you angry with me for being so stupid?'

Sam kept his gaze on the fire. Shelley suddenly realised that if Sam looked at her she'd be lost. She wondered if he was going to kiss her, and if so, what her reaction would be. She'd refuse, she decided. He might have saved her life, but he was a complete stranger, after all. Sam didn't turn his head towards her, but he spoke in a voice that was heady with passion.

'I'm wondering what you'd say if I asked if I could kiss you.'

He was asking permission! Shelley

was so charmed by his old-fashioned courtesy that she forgot all her sensible resolutions.

'I think that would be nice.'

She felt her breath catch in her throat as Sam finally turned his head to look at her. Her skin seemed to glow with excitement, and she thought she'd never forget this moment, the scent of ginger cordial and the softness of sheepskin, the crackling of the fire and the tang of wood smoke. Her lashes fluttered closed and her head tilted backwards, but the expected touch on her lips never came. Instead, Sam reached for her hand and turned it over as if he was reading the future in her palm.

'There's more you're not telling me. Are you hoping that Brent will come after you, that your absence will make him realise how much he cares?'

'He never really cared for me.'

Sam's hand settled on Shelley's shoulder in a sympathetic gesture that felt so natural. He was a stranger who stirred up disturbing sensations in her, yet his touch was as comforting as a long-time lover's. Shelley turned away from him and looked into the heart of the fire. It was easy to confess her deepest feelings to a man who listened so carefully. As she spoke, she felt the splash of healing tears on her cheeks.

'At first I was delighted that Brent loved the company so much. I thought that if he assumed more responsibility, I could find my own path more easily, perhaps finish my degree. I let him take over because I wasn't sure how much I cared about the company, and it made my father so happy. Even when Brent's interest turned into an obsession, I thought it was a phase that would pass.'

Sam's voice was so soft she could barely hear it.

'Would you like to go home and find the old Brent waiting for you?'

'There never was an old Brent. I fell in love with an image.'

A lump rose in her throat as she voiced the conclusion her thoughts over the past few days had forced her to reach.

'An illusion, a lie. I think he's been using me and milking the company.'

Sam's hand tightened on her shoulder and she felt him shift behind her and draw closer. She turned her head, blindly seeking the warmth and support of his body. Her hands met the solidness of his wide shoulders and her fingers twined in the soft strength of his thin sweater. A few tears welled from her eyes, but the expected storm of sobbing never materialised. Instead she felt a fire growing within her. The sensation of mystical contact returned in full force. Shelley knew that she wanted Sam to kiss her. She'd wanted him to kiss her since she'd opened her eyes that morning and met the concern in his brown eyes, felt the strength of his commitment to her well-being. She felt alive with anticipation as his mouth claimed hers.

She relished the heart-stopping moment as she felt the brush of his lips along the sensitive skin of her throat. Her fingertips touched the back of his neck. Her body melted under his kiss and she drew him closer to her. Her shocked mind framed a protest, but cold reason wilted and faded, leaving her free to kiss him with passion.

He was a man in a million and she wanted him. It was Sam who pulled away.

'No, Shelley, no. We mustn't do this.'

4

Sam felt as if his heart was being ripped from his body as he pulled away from Shelley, but he knew that he had no right to love her. He hadn't planned to woo her, but the sheen of tears in her amazing eyes and the sad tilt to her sweet mouth had undone him and made him kiss her. And with that one touch had come desire, pure and simple, astonishing in its power.

So many entanglements lay between them. She was engaged, he had been hired by her fiancé to find her, and most importantly of all, he was lying to her.

'Sam?' she said dreamily.

The husky intimacy in her soft voice nearly overturned his good resolutions. She was lying back in the soft whiteness of the sheepskins, looking up at him.

'I don't want to take advantage of you.'

Shelley's body tensed, then she rolled away from him and sat up hugging her knees in a graceful, feminine movement.

'I know what I'm doing,' she replied.

Sam's body ached with the longing to hold on to her, but he held firm.

'We're getting too involved. I don't want to fall into that trap.'

'I didn't ask for any promises.'

'You should! You deserve a man who'll never let you down.'

She lifted her head then, and looked at him very openly with those heartbreaking violet eyes.

'You saved my life.'

'I'm a doctor and I say this is madness. You were in a serious accident last night. You must go to bed and rest.'

Shelley turned her gaze away and gave him a sad smile. He saw the smooth curve of her throat as she swallowed and tried to sound casual.

'Oh, well, so you're going to play the medical card.'

She stood up and brushed down her clothes.

'Good-night, Sam. Put another log on the fire if you're staying up.'

Sam listened to her footsteps as she climbed the wooden stairs, then he rolled over and buried his face in his arms with a groan. How had he become involved in this incredible tangle? How could he tell Shelley that they'd only met because the man she was engaged to had hired Sam to find her? Sam knew that he'd always be thankful that he had met Shelley, but he wished that Brent Dughall could conveniently fall down to the bottom of a deep, dark, inescapable pit and rot there.

★ ★ ★

'Go to the devil, Dughall!'

Brent Dughall glared at the mobile phone in his hand and wished he could throttle the loud mouth on the other end — the man was working for him after all. He should show more respect.

'I only asked how you were getting on,' Brent repeated.

'And I told you not to bug me with phone calls.'

Brent looked at the computer terminal glowing on the desk in front of him. He had spent all morning going over the company figures. There was no way he could go back now. Thanks to the latest stock market crash, he didn't have enough money to repay what he'd taken in the first place. If only Shelley had kept her stupid nose out of his plans. He had absolutely no choice but to go forward. The chaos caused by her disappearance would buy him more time.

Unless he could get his hands on the loans for the expansion he wouldn't be able to liberate enough money from the bakery for him to live on in the Caribbean. He was investing more cautiously now, but safer investments netted lower returns. He had to have more money, and for that he had to have more time, and for that he had to have Shelley well out of his way.

'I'm worried about the time factor. What if she decides to come home and raise the alarm,' he asked.

'No chance of that, man. She's holed up with a boyfriend.'

'Impossible!'

'Sorry, man. I've tracked her down and seen them together.'

Brent felt furious. The lying, cheating shrew! She deserved to die.

'What kind of accident will you arrange?'

'We're not arranging nothing, man. I keep telling you that.'

Once again the hippie's caution reassured Brent. He'd been told the man was a professional, and that he'd never been caught.

'I'll leave it with you,' Brent agreed. 'I'll ring you later for a progress report.'

'And disturb me in the middle of something important? No, man. I'll tell you when it's over.'

'It's got to look natural.'

'All the best accidents do.'

Brent ended the call and went back to his computer. He could feel pressure building inside his head, urging him to hurry up, to take the money and get out. Should he leave Shelley to her lover and cut and run before he got in too deep?

He examined the total sum of money he'd salted away so far, and shook his head. It wasn't enough. He'd set himself targets and there was no way he was going to settle for less. As Brent remembered that Shelley was with another man, his last feelings of resistance evaporated. She deserved what was coming to her — all of it.

★   ★   ★

Shelley hugged her arms around her knees and looked at the snowy scene below. The window seat on the landing wasn't the warmest spot in the cottage, but it was a great place to sit and think.

She didn't think Sam knew this window overlooked the woodpile, where he'd already sawn a great heap of logs. Now he was using an axe to chop kindling. Chips flew around the shining blade. As many scattered in the snow as went in the basket, confirming Shelley's suspicion that Sam was working to relieve his feelings rather than to replenish the woodpile.

She wished she'd thought of wood-chopping herself. Her whole body had been aching when she woke up that morning, and she knew it wasn't whiplash from the crash. It was the aftermath of the tension she'd experienced in Sam's arms. She hadn't known that she was capable of such passion. It certainly made her decision to break her engagement easy. Shelley felt no regrets about cancelling her wedding at all.

What troubled her now were her suspicions about Brent's honesty. She wanted to talk to her father, but it was hardly a discussion they could have from a pay phone. It wasn't going to be much easier face to face. He wouldn't want to believe that Brent was stealing from him. She found it hard to believe herself. Maybe she was wrong. She should go back to the bakery and check all the figures, get some hard evidence before she starting throwing wild accusations, and for legal reasons, she'd better keep the matter to herself.

Shelley leaned closer to the cold glass and watched Sam bending to collect the scattered chips. He looked like a lumberjack in his red-check shirt and blue jeans — a fit, muscled, healthy lumberjack. She remembered the feel of his wide shoulders and the strength in his arms as he held her. She should go home, but how could she leave Sam?

She couldn't bear the thought of them driving off in opposite directions, never to meet again. Too much unfinished business lay between them. She wanted to solve the mystery that she felt he was concealing from her. She wanted to plumb the depths of his heart and find out if he cared for her. But most of all, she was afraid to leave because if the magical connection between them was born of the unusual circumstance that had brought them together and she would never experience it again, then she didn't want life to revert to normal and have that wonderful connection severed. She wanted to stay here for ever, in this cottage, with Sam.

Sam's pent-up energy was indeed being relieved as he swung the axe. He liked the way his physical exertions warmed his body, despite the cold air, and he liked the feel of the warm sun on his face. It was great to be outside. Breakfast had been impossible. Casual conversational topics had died away into the air between them, which was alive with the awareness of what wasn't being said.

Clearing away after the meal was worse. They'd spent more time bumping into each other and apologising than washing up. He had to get away before he went crazy. But he didn't want to leave, any more than he'd wanted to show his love to Shelley the previous evening. Sam wished he could have overcome his qualms, then at least he would have had extraordinary memories to take away with him. But it wasn't in him to cheat on a woman, and Shelley would be devastated if she discovered how much he'd lied to her.

Sam wielded the axe with vigour, allowing himself a private fantasy in which he confessed and Shelley forgave him and they lived happily ever after, but then reality intruded. The obstacles between them were insurmountable. Even if Shelley officially broke off her engagement and became free, even if she forgave his lies and agreed to see him again, then what? Their lives lay worlds apart.

She was a top executive, and she expected her hard work to be rewarded by a rich corporate lifestyle. He was going to be a busy doctor with a hospital salary and a medic's lifestyle. The discrepancy in their incomes didn't worry him, but the discrepancy in lifestyles was a barrier he couldn't see beyond.

A doctor's wife married the job as well as the man. She had to put up with the long hours, the unfair demands, the stress. Sam dropped the axe in the snow and stood with both hands on his hips wondering if he was serious. Marriage? He was thinking of marriage to Shelley? Impossible! He'd only known her two days.

He bent to collect the kindling he'd just finished splitting. His fingers turned red with cold as he picked wood chips out of the snow, and he realised how hard he must have been hitting the block from the distance that some of the splinters had travelled.

He moved in a wide circle around the chopping block, making regular trips to stack the kindling in a neat pile next to the logs he'd chopped earlier. Then he straightened and had a last look around to see if he'd missed any. Right at the boundary of the cottage garden, a dark stain in the snow caught his attention. It was a cigarette end and, beside it, footprints in the snow.

Curious, and faintly uneasy, Sam crunched his way over the deep snow to look at the prints. One person wearing large wellington boots had crossed the moors towards the house. Sam shaded his eyes with his hands and looked out over the snowy expanse, wondering if he should try to track the footprints, then he heard the diesel engine of a mini-tractor rumbling up the road. Sam walked around the front of the cottage in time to see a young, spotty-faced man clambering off the back of the red vehicle. The student professor headed for the cottage door. Mr Hawthorne walked towards Sam.

'Re-stocking my wood pile, I see.'

Sam smiled at the farmer.

'You're a good detective. Come

round the back and see what you make of some footprints.'

Mr Hawthorne examined the prints carefully, then he lifted his head and Sam saw anger glinting in the dark eyes under the man's busy grey brows.

'Sheep thieves, I'll bet. Folk as think it's clever to let another man do all the work and then waltz off with the profits as calm as you please. I've had trouble with them before.'

'Is there anything you can do?'

'I'll warn the local constable, and keep an eye out myself, and you stick close to that lass of yours. These folks can be ruthless.'

'I will,' Sam said soberly.

The young professor came around the side of the cottage, followed by Shelley. Sam felt the familiar deep pull of desire as he watched her. Her hair shone in the sunshine and her purple sweater was a bright splash against the snow. She hadn't bothered to put on a coat, despite the cold air. She was hugging her arms around her to keep warm. She greeted Mr Hawthorne with a soft, glowing smile.

'As it's my last evening, would you and Mrs Hawthorne like to come around and help me eat up the contents of the fridge before I go?'

'Aye, lass, we could do that.'

Shelley turned to Sam.

'Would you like to join us?'

'I thought you were leaving today.'

'Well, I've paid for the cottage until tomorrow, and it's getting a bit late to sort out a taxi and a train ticket, and there's all that food to eat up. I just thought, well, I thought, why not have a lovely evening tonight and set off tomorrow? But if you're busy, and you want to get going, well, we'll understand that. I expect you have lots more important things to do.'

She jammed her hands into the pockets of her jeans and hunched her shoulders defensively, as if preparing for a refusal. Sam's heart melted at the gesture. He pushed aside his common-sense worries about the danger of spending more time with Shelley. A picture of those mysterious footprints in the snow rose in his mind. It was his duty to protect her.

'Dinner sounds great,' he accepted.

5

Shelley reached into the washing-up bowl and pulled a blue willow-patterned dinner plate out of the suds.

'That's the last one.'

Mrs Hawthorne took the plate in her capable hands and dried it briskly.

'Many hands make light work.'

Sam wandered into the kitchen and picked up the coffee pot. Shelley felt a burning ache in her heart as his brown eyes met hers. She wished she could say something light and sparkling to show that he didn't affect her. Mrs Hawthorne smiled approvingly after Sam's departing figure.

'A good-looking doctor who can cook like an angel!' she sighed. 'My dear, I think you're going to be very happy with that young man.'

Shelley looked down at her hands which were covered in soap suds. Mrs

Hawthorne wouldn't be able to see that she'd taken off her engagement ring, but she turned to look into the kind hazel eyes of the farmer's wife. She'd better explain that Sam wasn't her fiancé.

'It's not that simple.'

Mrs Hawthorne interrupted with a jolly laugh.

'Relationships never are, my dear. But don't worry if you've run into a sticky patch. Love will see you through.'

'Sam doesn't love me.'

'Rubbish! Look at the way he looks at you! You'll be wanting some time alone if you've had a tiff. I'll take the men home.'

The farmer's wife bustled into the living-room before Shelley could stop her. Mr Hawthorne stood up at once, but the young professor was happily ensconced in a comfortable chair by the fire. He would have carried on telling Sam all about the university courses he was taking, but Mrs Hawthorne was firm.

'Come along, dear. There's a sight more snow coming tonight and I want to be safely in my bed long before it starts.'

Shelley and Sam stood side by side on the doorstep waving their guests out into the cold night air. The first few flakes of the promised snow drifted down. Shelley felt tension growing between them as they turned back into the empty cottage. She tried to keep her voice casual.

'I'm glad you're not driving in this weather. It's much better to set off in the morning.'

Sam flashed her a brief smile that sent electricity blasting around her system. Then he looked away from her as if the eye contact had burned him, and busied himself stacking the last few coffee cups. He didn't look at her as he spoke.

'And I'm glad you've agreed to let me drive you home. We all know what snow does to the public transport system.'

Shelley hovered by the foot of the stairs, knowing she was courting danger, but unable to tear herself away from his handsome face and well-loved figure.

'I suppose I'd better go to bed,' she said reluctantly.

Sam dropped the coffee cups with a clatter. His eyes looked very bright.

'Shelley, darling, Shelley!'

The very strength of her own desire was a warning.

'Good-night!' she said hastily, and fled upstairs and away from danger.

Some time later, she woke from a heavy, unpleasant sleep. Her head was stuffy and aching and there was a vile taste in her mouth.

'Shelley,' a deep voice cried in her ear. 'Wake up! There's a fire!'

She felt the slap of a wet towel as it landed on her face. She pushed it away with arms that felt limp and heavy. Sam took hold of her by the shoulders and he shook her.

'Cover your nose and mouth. You

mustn't breathe any more smoke.'

His constant shaking and calling were bringing her round. Shelley held the wet towelling to the lower part of her face and opened her eyes. The room was full of black smoke. She started coughing as soon as she saw it. Sam bent over her.

'Can you get up?'

She nodded and got out of the bed. His strong arms held her close as he urged her to hurry out of the room and down the stairs. At the open front door, he took a few seconds to help her push her bare feet into his wellington boots.

'Stay there!' he commanded, and vanished.

Shelley stood holding on to the door, looking out, breathing in cold air. A fire in the cottage, and Sam had saved her! But where had he gone? She breathed in more fresh air and felt her head clearing by the second. He'd gone back to fight the fire, of course! Shelley took hold of the wet towel and tied it firmly over her nose and mouth. Then she

102

reached behind the door for the fire extinguisher she knew stood there.

The fire wasn't in the living-room. The fire in the hearth was nearly out, only a few coals glowing peacefully in the grate, but the kitchen door stood open and dense black smoke swirled through the opening. Shelley hefted the fire extinguisher and ran through the open door. At first, she was bewildered to see Sam's dark figure jumping up and down in the smoke, but then she realised he was beating out flames with a wet blanket.

'What kind of fire is it?' she cried.

'Chip pan.'

The extinguisher held foam. Shelley blessed her luck. She pulled out the release pin, then directed the white spray towards the cooker top. The wet foam cut through the black smoke, and she could see that Sam had been piling soaked tea towels on top of the open chip pan, smothering the blaze. The foam took care of the few flames that were left. White suds piled up over the pan and dripped down the side of the cooker.

Shelley could hear hot metal sizzling as the cool liquid struck it. The units above the cooker were twisted and melted, but the fire was definitely out. She dropped the spent extinguisher. Her chest was tight with the acrid smell and the fumes, and she started to cough so hard that her throat hurt. Sam's angry face loomed through the smoke.

'I told you to stay outside!'

She felt his warm hands checking her face, her body.

'Are you OK?'

'I can't breathe.'

He drew her out of the kitchen and back to the open front door. She felt a finger pressing on her lips and his voice spoke right into her ear.

'Stay here a minute. Don't move.'

She heard his footsteps crunching over the snow as he sped away lightly. She stood in the dark, feeling puzzled. Where had he gone? Could the fire have spread outside? Should she find another extinguisher and run after him? She'd used up all the foam on the kitchen, but there was a water-based extinguisher on the landing.

Shelley shivered all over. For the first time she realised she was standing in the snow wearing nothing but a flimsy nightdress and Sam's wellington boots, but the cold air was clearing her head once more, and her thoughts were more chilling than any ice could be as she remembered that the kitchen of Mr Hawthorne's holiday cottage had never had a chip pan!

She ran out into the open space between the front of the cottage and the road. The snow-covered ground gave off a luminous glow under the dark sky. She had no idea where Sam might be. She held her breath, listening hard for any trace of him. All she could hear was her heart thudding in her ears. A few snowflakes drifted down and it was so quiet she imagined that she heard them touch the ground.

She was shaking all over. She drew in

another freezing lungful of air and held it, standing quiet, listening. She didn't dare call for Sam. She stood silent, her muscles quivering with fear and cold.

Sanity returned, and she decided to return to the cottage and find a coat, but as she placed her foot on the doorstep she felt a movement in the air behind her. She came to a snapping halt and opened her mouth to scream. A strong hand covered her face and muffled the sound before it could escape. Arms held her back with a solid strength she couldn't resist. It was a strength she recognised. She turned in the grip of her powerful captor and dissolved in his embrace.

'Hush,' Sam said quickly. 'Listen!'

She heard it now — the engine of a big car or van some distance away, turning over, the starter motor refusing to catch in the cold air. Then the engine fired and she heard it revving hard and then gunning away. The vehicle seemed to travel quickly into the night. Sam waited until the last sound died.

'Which way would you say it went?'

'Past the Hawthorne's farm and towards the main road.'

'Good girl. That's what I thought, too.'

He stirred as if he would have moved away. Shelley held on to his elbow.

'Did you see anyone?'

Sam's tone was regretful.

'I heard someone running away.'

Shelley was glad he hadn't been fighting in the dark. Sam turned to look at her, and in the glimmer of the snowlight she saw a mark on his cheek. Her fingers fluttered to his face.

'You're hurt.'

Sam lifted one hand as if he would brush her off.

'It's nothing.'

But Shelley had felt the stickiness of blood under her fingers.

'That injury needs tending, now!'

Once inside the cottage Sam insisted on checking the site of the fire and all the other rooms for damage before he would listen to Shelley's questions.

'Do you want to call the fire brigade or the police?'

'We're phoneless,' Sam replied absently, and then his head swung around and he gave her a sharp look. 'Police?'

'I haven't got a chip pan, Sam. There wasn't one here.'

His eyes bored into Shelley's.

'Impossible.'

'I've got a secret passion for chips. I looked everywhere for one.'

'You must have made a mistake.'

'Sam, even if I was mistaken about the chip pan, which one of us put it on the stove and left it to overheat? Was it you? It certainly wasn't me.'

Sam turned on his heel and scanned the living-room. Then he walked over to the foot of the wooden stairs. He reached up and fiddled with the smoke detector that was fixed to the wall. He came back to Shelley holding a small battery in his hand.

'Do you know if Mr Hawthorne keeps spares?'

'In the top drawer of that dresser.'

Sam rummaged through maps and local walks, instructions for the central heating, fuse wire and light bulbs before finding a packet of batteries and a tester. The one he'd taken out of the smoke detector was dead. It was also a different brand from the ones in the packet. Shelley looked at the evidence.

'That doesn't prove anything,' she said almost to herself.

Sam took a fresh battery and inserted it into the smoke alarm.

'All right. Let's ring the police.'

Shelley met his eyes.

'You were here, Sam, and you know me, yet you're half inclined to think it must be an accident. The police would think I was a lunatic. I've changed my mind: Let me look at your injury instead.'

Sam insisted on securing the house and setting the burglar alarm before he would go upstairs. Shelley followed him into the bedroom he'd been using and made him sit on the bed.

'It's nothing,' Sam protested. 'I can see to it.'

'And deprive me of a chance to boss you around for a change?' Shelley asked him, as she collected up cotton wool and found some antiseptic.

She had to move very close to him to reach the cut on his cheek. The hand that was holding the bowl of warm water trembled slightly and Shelley had to remind herself to concentrate on the task in hand.

'How did you hurt yourself?'

Sam winced and then laughed.

'I ran into a branch of the apple tree by the gate. Not much of a hero.'

She looked at the perfect lines of his face in the soft glow of the bedside lamp and imprinted every detail on her mind. She wanted to keep Sam's picture in her thoughts for ever. She wished she could express a fraction of the emotions that boiled in her heart.

'Then how come I owe you my life twice over?'

Sam lifted his head and his

chocolate-brown eyes met hers. He lifted one hand and touched her hair lightly.

'Go to bed, Shelley.'

The dark frustration in his voice rang in her ears. She stood up obediently. She even took a step to the door, but then she realised that she couldn't be without him that night, their last night.

She turned. Sam was still sitting on the side of the bed, watching her. She crossed the room rapidly and kneeled on the floor, the folds of her nightdress fluttering around her. She looked up at him.

'Kiss me.'

She was afraid that he'd draw back, say something sensible and send her away, but instead he caught her up swiftly and the magic of his kiss left her breathless. Then he tilted her face and tipped it up so that he could look at her closely.

'Are you sure about this?' he asked.

A sweet shudder ran through her as she met his gaze. She could see her own longing mirrored in the brown depths of his eyes. She pressed a palm to his cheek.

'No regrets.'

He clasped her hand and turned it over, pressing a kiss into the palm, slowly, reverently, lovingly. Shelley was aware of a sharp pain in her heart that cut through the sweetness of the moment. She wished the man in her arms could love her the way she loved him, but at least she'd have sweet memories to take her through the rest of her life.

His arms wrapped around her, as his mouth claimed hers.

6

Sam tooted the horn of his Jeep in farewell as he and Shelley drove out of the Hawthornes' farm yard.

'Nice people,' he said.

Shelley sat back in her seat.

'We shouldn't have stayed for lunch.'

Sam glanced at her.

'Are you worried about the weather? We should be home before dark.'

Shelley patted her stomach and laughed.

'There are too many calories in farmhouse roast beef.'

'You don't need to worry about calories,' Sam said, wondering how he could ever have written off Shelley as not his type. 'Men love curves.'

She turned her head and looked out of the window.

'Here comes that snow we were promised.'

She was right to change the subject, Sam thought. His last remark had skated too close to danger. An insatiable longing tugged at his heart. It seemed hard that he'd never again know the sweet contentment he'd found in her arms, yet what could he do? He cast a glance at Shelley's left hand. At least she'd left off the ring, but the sight of that dimpled white hand depressed him. It reminded him of the difference between his own tanned and muscled hands and hers, the difference in their lifestyles.

The difference that meant that their affair was over, despite his feeling that it hadn't even begun. No regrets, she'd said, as they'd kissed and held each other, but he had a million of them, starting with the lies he'd told her. He turned on to the motorway and drove quite a long way in silence. Shelley stirred beside him.

'It's snowing pretty hard now. Do you think it'll blow over?'

Sam looked out of the window.

Flakes whirled around the windscreen in a hypnotic winter ballet, but the heater was blasting hot air around their legs, giving the illusion of cosiness, and the engine was pulling strongly.

'We'll be all right on the motorway, but I think it's going to go dark very early.'

Shelley's brows drew together in a frown. Sam looked at her.

'Worried? We can pull over if you like.'

'I was thinking about all the insurance forms I'll have to fill in when I get back.'

'The Hawthornes were very good about the damage to their cottage. Did you notice they didn't seem surprised? It makes me wonder if there was a chip pan in the kitchen after all.'

Shelley groaned.

'I keep wondering if I was mistaken, but the fire still doesn't make sense. Who was making chips in the middle of the night? A peckish ghost?'

Sam rubbed his eyes. Driving

through the whirling snow was tiring, and he'd slept lightly last night, if at all, alert for danger, puzzling over the very same questions himself. There were no easy answers, and he didn't want to worry her.

'Forget it,' he advised.

Shelley gave him an unexpectedly wicked glance, and her tone was more than suggestive.

'And lose all those good memories?'

Sam looked at her quickly before turning his attention back to the road. He had to stay alert. They could still be in danger. He had to figure out what was going on. He wished he was a real detective. A warning hunch deep inside told him that the fire had not been set off by accident, or by a poltergeist, or even a sheep thief! He remembered Shelley's throwaway remark two nights ago about her fiancé stealing from the company. He was tempted to ask for more details, but it wouldn't be too hard for her to follow his train of thought, and honestly, it sounded so improbable.

The man had been so worried about Shelley that he'd hired Dwayne's agency to find her, and Dughall still didn't know where his fiancée was. They had driven past several motorway service stations with perfectly good pay phones, but Sam had not felt right about stopping at any of them and phoning in his report, so how could Brent Dughall have anything to do with Sam's increasing feeling of danger?

Shelley felt shut out as she scanned Sam's withdrawn expression. She'd felt he was keeping secrets from her the first time they'd met. He was concentrating on the road, naturally, given the worsening weather conditions, but she could feel that mental shutters were in place, hiding his thoughts from her. She looked at her watch. It was only two o'clock, but the dark snow clouds made it seem like late evening.

She'd be home soon, she thought. She'd make up with her father, and then upset him again by cancelling her wedding, but there was no way she could continue with the businesslike arrangement that had seemed so practical before, not now she'd had a taste of paradise. She looked at the strong face of the man next to her. Maddening, secretive, he was so cool and reserved, but she couldn't forget the breathtaking exhilaration of his tenderness. How could she let him walk away once the magic of his love had touched her? She had to try. Even if he knocked her back, she had to say something.

'Sam, when we get back, do you think we'll see anything of each other?'

She saw a flash of astonishment in his eyes as he glanced away from the road and at her. It could only have been a second before he looked back through the snowy windscreen. Then he shouted.

'Hold on, Shelley!'

Sam couldn't believe the road in front of him. Within the split second he'd been looking at Shelley, a rusty blue van had veered into his lane. Sam took his foot off the accelerator. The van was weaving dangerously in front of him. Sam touched his brake lightly, aware of the dangers of skidding, and leaned on the horn to let the vehicle know Sam was close behind him. He saw a ruby glow as the van's brake lights came on, but he had no option other than to swerve violently into the middle lane. He saw snow spraying from the tyres of the van as it, too, changed lanes. Beside him, Shelley stirred, and he registered the shocked tones of her voice.

'He's after us! Oh, no, Sam! He's doing this on purpose.'

Even after all his naval training and his time in Africa, Sam couldn't believe that he was under attack, but Shelley was right. The blue van lurched dangerously. It was so difficult to brake in the snow, and Sam was running out of road. It took all his skill to swerve the Jeep into the slow lane and steer it into a gap in the traffic between an oil tanker and a delivery van. The blue van nipped into the space behind him and this time Sam felt an impact on the rear of the Jeep. The van driver was ramming his Jeep, hoping to make them crash! Sam felt anger rising, a primitive urge to take on the driver and make him pay for his dangerous antics, but he had Shelley's safety to consider.

Sam then steered the Jeep out of the slow lane and on to the hard shoulder. The van followed close behind and then, as Sam was braking, the van accelerated and drove into Sam on the right side, crashing so hard into the front wing of the Jeep that the whole vehicle spun around in a sickening loop before coming to rest with its nose buried in a snowdrift at the foot of the motorway embankment.

Sam twisted in his seat, scanning the road, afraid that the van driver was insane enough to turn around and come back to crash into the Jeep again, but he saw the rusty vehicle a good distance ahead, pulling into the lane of the slowly-moving vehicles and vanishing from sight, swallowed up in the stream of motorway traffic. Sam instantly turned his attention to Shelley, praying that he hadn't hurt her. The face that she turned to him was pale, and her violet eyes were wide with shock.

'That was deliberate.'

Sam still didn't want to believe it.

'There are some mad drivers in the world.'

Shelley's face quivered and she seemed to be about to argue, but then she pulled herself together and looked out of the window. She even managed a laugh.

'How about that? We crashed right next to an emergency phone!'

As he switched on the hazard lights and rummaged in the boot for the red warning triangle, Sam admired Shelley's spirit. He used the emergency phone and then walked back, feeling the cold brush of snow against his face as he returned to the Jeep. Shelley jumped out of the passenger door to meet him. She was the most beautiful woman he'd ever met, he thought, as she crunched over the deep snow towards him. She looked down at her feet and then up at his face and met his gaze very openly.

'I'm leaving Brent. We're through!'

Despite the heavy rumble of the traffic that swept past them, Sam had heard every word. He felt a hot wave of longing and suppressed it at once. He'd already nearly killed her in a car accident, and if he didn't keep his wits about him, she'd now freeze. Emotions had no place in an emergency situation. He reached out and grasped her shoulders.

'We're under too much immediate pressure to talk about the future.'

She continued to look at him with that intent violet gaze.

'It's not because of you.'

He saw crystal liquid well up in the corners of her fabulous eyes. They blazed violet out of her pale face. She was so gorgeous that he had to reach out and touch her. As his finger brushed her cheek, he felt her tremble.

'I don't know what I'm trying to say to you,' she said.

Sam drew her close. He knew it was crazy to take her in his arms. Stranded on the edge of a busy motorway in a snowstorm was no place for love-making, but the sweet pain of knowing their time together was nearly over forced him to reach for her. Reason slipped away, his awareness of the danger around them faded, and he bent his head and kissed her.

She responded with no hesitancy at all. Her lips parted confidently, she wove her fingers into his hair and pressed the soft curves of her body against him, pulling him, holding him closer. A stinging shower of snow hit his back and sprayed down his neck. Sam looked up to see a bright yellow snow plough thundering by. He became aware of the roar of the traffic, and that Shelley was shivering in the cold. He drew her towards the Jeep.

'Take off that silly coat.'

'It's not very waterproof,' Shelley admitted, throwing the sodden garment on to the front seat.

'Have this sweater. It's very warm.'

She pulled the cream wool over her head and breathed deeply. Sam looked at the happiness glowing in her eyes and brushed a few snowflakes from her wet hair.

'This is a mistake.'

She shook her head.

'I feel so alive.'

Sam pulled her to him, wrapping his arms around the precious figure in the oversized sweater. Her head nestled on his shoulder. She felt so sweet and warm in his arms. He nuzzled her ear, and then couldn't help pressing a tender kiss to her neck. Her head tipped back and he heard her low murmur.

'I think I love you,' she whispered.

Sam was stunned. He looked up and

away over the snowbound motorway. She was so brave, so honest in her feelings. There were so many obstacles, but he longed to believe they could have a future together. As he stared out at the thickly-falling snow, he sensed rather than saw a vehicle approaching them. Sam's whole body went on alert, but fluorescent paint and flashing lights quickly identified a tow truck. A man and a woman got out, bulky in their rescue jackets. The man gave Sam a wink and a grin.

'Kissing is a good way of keeping warm on a snowy night.'

Sam and Shelley moved apart, but Sam kept hold of her hand as he spoke to the rescue crew.

'I guess you'll be busy tonight.'

The female dug in her large pockets for a clipboard that held some different coloured sheets of paper.

'You can say that again. Sign here, please, and we'll take you to the next services.'

Sam regarded her in dismay.

'But we're on our way to Manchester.'

She shook her head.

'You're only covered to the nearest garage.'

'Dwayne, you cheap skate!' Sam muttered, then he asked directly, 'Could we come to any other arrangement?'

The man looked regretful.

'Sorry, mate, we're on a contract. We can't take private jobs. But don't worry, you can sort it all out from the services.'

Sam bowed to the inevitable.

'At least we'll be off this road.'

A motorway service café had never looked so warm and brightly welcoming. Sam looked into Shelley's cold face as they walked inside.

'I think we should have a hot drink before we do anything,' he suggested.

Shelley smiled up at him.

'And something to eat. I thought lunch would hold me for hours, but I'm hungry again.'

Sam felt a lot better after open-topped sandwiches, Danish pastries and hot coffee. Shelley was burrowing in her handbag. She pulled out her phone and frowned at it.

'Can you believe it? I left it switched on and now the battery is flat.'

Sam got his phone out of his pocket and pushed it over to her.

'Use mine.'

'But you have to arrange about the car and everything. You'd better preserve the battery.'

'I'll use the pay phone,' Sam said gallantly.

He stood up before she could argue any further. He'd do a lot more for Shelley than use a phone in the lobby, he reflected, as he walked towards the bank of pay phones and when he'd finished his calls he was going to tell her so. A taxi proved easy enough to arrange, but when he phoned Dwayne, things became more difficult.

'An operative should never be out of touch with the office,' his friend bellowed. 'You're nuts, do you know that? I've been worried sick about you. Where on earth have you been?'

'Finding Shelley Rushton,' Sam said, his original pride in his achievement coming back to him. 'In fact, I'm with her now.'

'I shouldn't have let you play detective! You should never get involved with a client.'

Sam chuckled.

'I'm in deeper than you think, Dwayne. She's quite a girl.'

He could hear the expression in his friend's voice.

'I shudder to think what might have happened to you. Good job this was a simple case with no danger involved.'

Sam held the receiver silently for a few seconds, then he decided he'd better confess. Despite his wild imaginings the night before, in the cold light of day, as he told Dwayne about the fire and the motorway incident, he was now sure they were accidents. Dwayne was silent for a long moment. Then he spoke thoughtfully.

'If you had called in to your answer service, or looked at your text messages, or even rung me every day as originally instructed, then you would have known that Brent Dughall has called us off the case.'

Sam's first reaction was relief.

'Then he can't be involved.'

Dwayne's chuckle was wry.

'You're too pure to live in this wicked world, Sammy, boy. What if Brent Dughall hired a hit man to follow you?'

Guilt burned into Sam's soul. It couldn't be his fault that Shelley was in danger.

'It can't be true. What possible motive could he have?'

'You'd be surprised why people kill. Brent could want Shelley dead so that he can marry another woman, or he might be plotting an insurance scam, or he might be planning to take her place as daddy's heir to the company. He might even be trying to hide the fact he's been embezzling, or he might be the type to seek revenge for something, or he could be — '

'Stop!' Sam cried. 'Shelley told me she suspected Brent had been stealing from the company, but she didn't seem very sure about it.'

Dwayne's tone was urgent.

'That'll be it. Don't let her go back to the house or the company until we've had a chance to debrief her at the agency. Get back to her now. She's in danger until you bring her in.'

Sam's hand was shaking as he replaced the receiver. The solid English gentleman in him recoiled at the melodrama of the situation. He turned over phrases in his mind as he walked back to the table where he'd left Shelley. What was the best way to tell her that her life was in danger and they must go to a private investigator's office at once?

It was an anti-climax to see the empty table. Sam perched on a chair, his body tense. He didn't even like the idea of her going to the cloakroom on her own. He wanted her near to him, close to him, so that he could protect her.

Then he saw that she'd left his phone lying on the table, almost as though it had been thrown down. Sam frowned. That was careless of her. Someone could have come along and stolen it. He tapped his fingers on the table, hating the waiting. He decided he'd distract himself by listening to his messages before she came back.

Sam reached out for his phone, but the second he picked it up and looked at the tiny screen he felt as if cold ice had been poured down his spine. Shelley couldn't access his answer service, even if she wanted to, because one needed a pin number, but Dwayne had sent text messages as well, now clearly scrolled across the screen for anyone to read.

Sam wanted to kill himself as he looked at the betraying words now displayed on the tiny screen. Shelley wouldn't need to be much of a detective herself to discover how much he'd lied to her. Sam raised his head and looked around the bright café and out through the now dark windows to the snowy carpark outside. He could feel his heart thumping and feel sick apprehension in the pit of his stomach. It was easy enough to deduce why Shelley had gone, but what he urgently needed to know was where she had gone, and how!

7

Shelley sat bolt upright in the cab of a Rushton's Bakery lorry. Luckily her employee liked to talk, so she didn't have to worry about keeping up a conversation, but her cheeks ached with smiling as the driver chatted on.

'Gee, it's too bad about your Range Rover, Miss Rushton. I bet you feel like someone's chopped your legs off, trying to get around without a car.'

'It's difficult,' she agreed. 'I was about to ring for a taxi when I recognised you. I couldn't believe my luck.'

'I'm always the last one back,' the driver said. 'That's because I do the longest run.'

She turned her head to look out at the dark night. From her seat in the high cab of the truck she could see empty white fields covered in snow.

Sam would have discovered that she'd gone by now. Would he be wondering where she was, or would he shrug philosophically and go on to his next job?

A cold shiver of disgust whirled inside her. A job, that's all she'd been to him. It made her sick to think of Sam talking to Brent Dughall about her, plotting, hunting her down and why on earth had Brent wanted her found?

The cab of the truck was remarkably quiet and luxurious. The driver's chatter floated in and out of her consciousness. She kept an expression that said she was listening frozen on her face, and made the odd comment, but her mind would not stop thinking about Sam.

She'd been such a fool. Why hadn't she listened to her instincts when she'd first seen the headlights following her that night? There had been other clues as well, like the time she'd found him going through her papers. But by then she'd been so besotted that she'd never even asked him what he'd been looking for.

Shelley clenched her fists as if the movement would relieve the pain in her heart. But what difference would a few questions have made? Sam was a wizard at concocting stories. She writhed inside as she thought of what a gullible fool she'd been. She'd been so touched and privileged when he'd shared his memories of Africa. It hurt to realise that Sam had been playing a cruel game of deceit with her.

Shelley shifted in her seat. It was torture to sit in this cab pretending to smile at the driver. She wished she was alone so that she could vent her feelings. She couldn't go home. She couldn't bear to face her father or Brent until she'd had a chance to pull herself together. She looked out of the window. They were driving through suburbs now. She waited for a gap in the driver's conversation.

'Can you drop me off at a train station?' she asked him.

His tone was full of surprise.

'Aren't you going back to the bakery?'

'Not yet.'

'I can drop you off at your house, if you like. We're not usually allowed to make detours, but you are the boss, after all, and I've got plenty of time.'

'That's very kind of you, but I've a couple more days' holiday yet.'

'Ah, well, I see what you mean then. It does you good, a nice holiday. Me and the wife, we're going to Tenerife again this year.'

Shelley wished she was truly on holiday. She'd like to rent Mr Hawthorne's cottage later in the year. The moors would be lovely in spring. To make it perfect, she'd have to take her own chip pan, but she'd be very careful how she used it! There'd be no Sam this time to rescue her if she set the place on fire. It was amazing how quickly her thoughts circled back to Sam. He'd seemed so sure that the kitchen fire and the murderous attack by the blue van were coincidences, but in reality he must be in trouble.

Perhaps a villain had a grudge against Sam and was determined to have revenge. She hoped he'd be all right, and then she changed her mind. She hoped they would catch him and make him suffer. Then maybe he'd get some idea of how his lies had made her feel.

The bakery truck stopped outside a train station with a sigh of air brakes. She thanked the friendly driver and climbed down the steps of the cab. He jumped down and fetched around the one small bag she'd taken with her when she fled. The driver looked at the dark brick building with misgiving.

'That station doesn't look very busy. I'll hang on, make sure you're all right. Trains might be off due to the weather.'

Shelley couldn't pretend to be happy for one more second, nor did she want anyone to know where she was going.

'It's only six o'clock. There'll be plenty of trains yet.'

'I'll take you to the ticket office.'

Shelley looked around her for inspiration.

'You're parked on double yellow lines. Better go.'

The driver looked chagrined.

'Well, if you're sure.'

'I'll be fine, and thank you very much.'

Shelley's tone had been more confident than she felt, but as she walked into the seemingly deserted station she began to see signs of life. The man behind the ticket window assured her that trains were running and asked her where she wanted to go. Shelley studied the timetable and then saw that the boat train was due in very shortly. It must be fate.

'One single to Conway in North Wales, please.'

★   ★   ★

Sam didn't know if he could believe what Dwayne was telling him.

'How can you be so sure that Shelley

hasn't gone home?'

The detective made a steeple of his fingers and looked at Sam over the top of them.

'I have my methods.'

'Don't mess me about, Dwayne. I've got to find her.'

Dwayne patted the bulky file that lay on his desk.

'These are the details the fiancé supplied. Did Shelley give you any clues as to where she might go? A friend, a favourite place?'

Sam felt vicious when he thought of Brent Dughall laying claim to Shelley.

'She's not engaged any more.'

Dwayne's eyebrows shot up.

'This sounds serious.'

'It is. Help me find her, Dwayne.'

'That's what I'm trying to do. Think back. Did she mention any friends?'

'She told me that she met her best friend at art college, but she never told me her surname, only that the woman lived in Wales. She had a name like a flower, Lily maybe, or Rose.'

Sam hit his forehead in frustration.

'This is hopeless. We'll never find her. I don't know where to start. Should we ring the art college and try to get a student list from them?'

Dwayne's voice was smug as he flicked through the papers in Brent's folder.

'Or should we try Heather Mills, Maes-y-Coedd Cottage, Conway, North Wales?'

Sam's head jerked up.

'How did you do that?'

'Easy, Sammy, boy. It only looks like magic to those who know nothing about the detective business.'

Sam felt utterly miserable as he realised how out of his depth he was.

'It was criminally insane of me to get involved. All I've done is put Shelley's life in danger.'

'If it comes to that, I'm the expert and I should never have sent you. But how could we have known that this seemingly simple case would prove so complex?'

'I feel so useless,' Sam replied.

Dwayne chuckled.

'A doctor can't say that! You're more use to society than I am.'

Sam jumped to his feet.

'Forget the philosophy. I'm going to Wales.'

Dwayne held up one hand.

'Whoa, boy. We don't know she's there yet.'

He picked up his desk phone and spoke briefly to his female assistant, Cindy. Sam's brain whirled as he listened to the conversation, but he didn't speak until Dwayne put down the receiver.

'How on earth do you expect Cindy to find out whether Shelley's at the cottage or not?'

'She's brilliant on the phone,' Dwayne said proudly. 'Even if Heather won't talk, our Cindy will ring around her neighbours until she finds someone who wants to chat. I've never known her fail.'

Sam paced Dwayne's office restlessly.

'I'd rather be doing something.'

'No point dashing off to Wales if the girl's gone to a Scottish health farm,' Dwayne told him. 'And here's Cindy back now. I told you she'd be quick.'

Cindy was smiling.

'I have a definite sighting of Shelley Rushton at the Welsh address.'

Sam could have kissed her. He grabbed up his coat.

'I need to hire a car.'

Dwayne held up that warning hand again.

'Calm down. I've arranged transport for you, and I'll spare you one of my team as an escort as far as the motorway turn-off for Wales. We don't want any unwanted hit men picking up Shelley's trail by following you.'

As Dwayne explained in detail how Sam should liaise with the operative who would help to make sure he wasn't followed, Sam was gripped by a growing feeling of unreality. He felt as if he was acting in a movie. It was hard to believe that Shelley could be in danger.

'I wish you could come with me, Dwayne.'

'Yeah, but you, myself and all my available staff are committed to this kidnap situation we've got ongoing at the moment. The moment it resolves, I'll come after you.'

Sam shook his friend's hand.

'I'm worried. What if I'm not up to it?' he said.

His friend replied stoutly.

'I've got a lot of faith in you, Sam. You're only doubting yourself because you're involved with the girl. Love does funny things to a man's judgment.'

And as Sam clattered down the agency stairs with the operative who would be driving with him in the second car, he could find nothing to argue against in Dwayne's summing-up of his mental state! Sam was in love all right. He only hoped he wouldn't be too late to tell Shelley so.

★   ★   ★

The fire in the vast open hearth of Heather's cottage had burned down to a pile of white ash and a few glowing embers by the time Shelley had spilled out her story to her friend. All she held back were her suspicions about Brent. She did tell her friend that she was breaking the engagement, but not why. Heather listened to every word, and made sure Shelley was talked out, before she stirred.

'Are you going to ring your father?'

'It's too complicated to explain on the phone, but I'll go home tomorrow and face the music. It's funny, I'm looking forward to getting back to work. I've missed the bakery.'

Heather's canny blue eyes examined Shelley's face.

'Because burying yourself in work is easier than facing up to your emotions?' she asked.

Shelley felt a hot flush sting her cheeks. Did Heather suspect that Shelley hadn't told her all there was to say about Sam? Shelley looked around

144

at the dark blue walls of the cottage. They were hung with gold-framed mirrors; loose white covers draped softly over the long sofas that stood around the fire; the gloss paint was dark green, the ceiling a bright pink. It should have looked dreadful, but it didn't. It looked wild and free and artistic, just like Heather herself. Shelley smiled at her friend.

'I was never a true artist like you. I resented being dragged away from art school, that's why I rebelled, but I know myself now. I love the bakery.'

Heather yawned and stretched, then she gave Shelley a sideways look.

'Just like you love Dr Private Investigator Gilday?'

'How can you say that? I told you the man betrayed me.'

'You're still wearing his sweater.'

Shelley's hands slipped over the over-sized wool. The warm fabric smelled faintly of Sam's aftershave. Maybe its warmth wasn't the only comfort it was bringing her, not that she wanted to admit that. She swallowed.

'Heather, he lied to me.'

'There are two sides to every story. It sounds to me like you ran out without giving him a chance to explain.'

Hurt clawed at Shelley's heart.

'I hate him.'

Heather's blue eyes examined Shelley's face with the deep, assessing look of an artist.

'That's not what your eyes are telling me.'

Shelley gave up the pretence. The emptiness inside her was too much to be borne alone. She drew her knees up on the sofa and wrapped her arms around them. She dropped her head and spoke without looking up.

'I wish I'd never found out the truth. Then I could have kept the memories.'

She felt Heather's hand caress her hair lightly.

'You're exhausted, and no wonder. It's three o'clock!'

'I'm sorry.'

'What are friends for? I'll make you a hot drink or you won't sleep. You can take it to bed with you.'

★　★　★

Sam was pleased to see light in the ground-floor windows of Heather's cottage. It was three o'clock on a fine, frosty morning. His mission was going to be difficult enough without having to wake up one woman he'd never met before and one who was furious with him.

He walked over the iron-hard ground to the cottage, but he hesitated before knocking on the door. It was imperative to get his story straight in his mind before he saw Shelley. He'd decided not to concentrate on personal issues. There was no easy way to explain the lies he'd told her. His task was to make her understand the danger she was in. She had very good reasons to mistrust him, but he had to make her believe him. Her life could depend on it. He lifted his fist and banged on the door.

Shelley's heart overflowed with painful emotions as she peered through the white curtains at the familiar figure standing on the step. His head was slightly tilted and his hands were in his pockets.

'It's Sam,' she whispered.

Heather uncurled herself from the sofa and sauntered towards the door.

'Now why am I not surprised?'

'Don't let him in!'

'I think you should talk to the man.'

Shelley listened as her friend unlocked the door. She wasn't ready to meet Sam. The house seemed to shrink around her as he crossed the threshold. He stood with his hands in his pockets, looking at her with eyes that seemed to burn into her soul. She couldn't move or breathe or swallow, until Heather's voice broke the spell.

'If you two will unlock your gaze for a moment so that I can get past you and reach the stairs, I'll go to bed.'

Sam spoke at once.

'I do apologise. We can't possibly drive you out of your own front room.'

Heather gave Sam a look that said she'd joined his fan club.

'I feel the need for a long, hot bath. You two can chat to each other in peace.'

Shelley could hear her voice shaking.

'Heather, come back. I have nothing to say to this man.'

Her friend ignored her and Shelley heard the firm footsteps growing fainter as Heather ascended the wooden stairs. Hot tears stung Shelley's eyes. She turned away. She didn't want Sam to know that he had the power to upset her. She walked over to the massive hearth. Sam followed her.

'I'd like to explain.'

Shelley leaned her head on the oak beam that acted as mantelpiece.

'You mean tell me a few more lies.'

She felt his hands grip her shoulders with terrifying strength. He spun her around to face him. She was stunned by the desperation she could feel emanating from his body. Red lights from the fire glittered in his brown eyes, and his voice was low and savage.

'You have to listen. This is not about me, it's about Brent Dughall. He's out to kill you, Shelley.'

Sam could see from her stunned face that he had her full attention, but the paleness of her cheeks and the shock he could see widening her eyes made him wish it didn't have to be this way. Her body was tense, as wary as a wild animal's, and he didn't blame her a bit.

She lifted her chin and faced him bravely. Sam felt admiration. She had good reason to think she was dealing with a lunatic, but her voice was firm and strong.

'What kind of mad story is this?'

'We think Brent Dughall hired a hit man to kill you.'

She stared at him, distrust shimmering in her eyes. Sam longed to hold her and kiss away her doubt, but that wasn't the way to approach her now. She was shaking her head in utter disbelief.

'You're insane.'

'You were right. The chip pan fire and the near smash on the motorway were not accidents.'

She looked away, frowning, and then back at Sam.

'None of this makes sense. I thought you were working for Brent. Why come to me with this mad story now?'

Sam's heart twisted.

'How can you think I'd work for a man like him? Brent Dughall used the agency to track you down, then had his hitman track me. He sacked the agency as soon as you were found.'

Shelley's lovely eyes were wide with confusion.

'It doesn't sound like a very workable plan to me.'

Sam shrugged.

'Even an experienced operative might not have spotted his plan, and Brent must have been delighted when good old amateur Sam Gilday bumbled along.'

'You're not a private investigator?'

'No. The friend I was staying with runs the agency. He suddenly had more work than his staff could handle, and there I was with time on my hands and an ego that said finding a missing woman would be simple for a smart guy like me.'

Shelley's huge eyes stared at him from beneath her dark lashes.

'Were you really in Africa?'

'Everything I told you was true, I swear it. Look, Shelley, come and sit down. We need to talk.'

Sam sat on the sofa, hoping she'd follow suit, but she was too tense to do more than perch on the arm of the couch. She wrapped her arms around her as if she were cold. Sam leaned forward and put a couple of logs on the embers of the fire, but he knew the temperature wasn't Shelley's true problem.

The pain and confusion she must be

feeling in her heart were clear to read on her face, and his conscience pinched him with hot daggers when he remembered how much of her agony was his fault. Flame licked around the new logs and he sat back on the sofa.

'You mentioned to me once that you suspected that Brent had been stealing from the company.'

Shelley looked down and muttered, 'How can I believe something so horrible?'

Then she lifted her head and raked her hands back through her hair. She looked directly at Sam, and he heard the desperate plea in her voice.

'I was engaged to him! You're asking me to believe that the man I was going to marry now wants me dead!'

Sam longed to ease the pain he could sense in her. He wanted so much to have things right between them that he forgot all commonsense and reached for her. Perhaps if he could touch her the magic they generated between them would take over and she'd believe him.

Shelley felt Sam's hands take her face, cradling it gently. She thought that she would cry, she so badly wanted to be in Sam's arms and know what he truly felt for her. She'd sensed all along that he'd told her some lies at the cottage, but his kisses had felt honest, and her instincts told her he was telling the truth now. If she could touch him, she would know. His face was in partial shadow.

He looked like a mysterious stranger, and yet she felt like she'd known him for ever. Impossible to believe that it was only three days since she'd first seen him. He held her face still, and his voice was so low that she had to strain to hear his whisper.

'I didn't mean to fall in love with you. I tried every way I knew how to stop, but it was impossible.'

His lips touched hers with a soft affection that touched her heart. He was holding himself back, waiting for her reaction, to see if she trusted him. Shelley longed to give herself entirely.

She wanted Sam's love to drive away her doubts, but even as she softened in his arms, the hurt she'd been holding tight inside her broke forth in sobs that tore at her chest and would not be stopped. Sam's cool fingers touched her wet cheeks, then he put comforting arms around her and rocked her as if she was a baby. His voice was a soothing murmur.

'It'll be all right.'

Shelley clung to the strength and the warmth of him. He held her like a rock until her tears eased off to the point where she could talk.

'I'm so confused. I don't know what to do.'

She felt him press a kiss on the top of her head, but then he gently unwound his arms and moved away from her.

'We're both confused because we don't know anything. Tomorrow we'll check out your suspicions. Whatever we find we'll be on firmer ground. Go on up to bed and get a few hours' sleep. I'll be fine on the sofa.'

8

They drove in silence until they came to the first road sign for Rushton's Bakery. Sam looked ahead at the bulk of the factory buildings and picked up his mobile phone.

'This is Sam. Is Dwayne back yet? We're in sight of the bakery.'

Sam listened briefly and then turned back to Shelley, a frown creasing his forehead.

'Dwayne's still on the kidnap case, but he rang the office again and left a message. On no account are we to enter the bakery.'

Shelley was bone weary and a headache throbbed at her temples. She'd stared for hours at her bedroom ceiling last night, feeling Sam's kiss on her lips and wondering if there could be any future for them. There was no relief for her tormented mind. If she stopped thinking about Sam, the disturbing idea that Brent was a thief and a murderer surfaced to torment her. It couldn't be true. She looked at the solid, familiar outline of the bakery and scowled.

'Rubbish. I've been here every day of my life, and it's broad daylight.'

Sam gave her a doubtful look, but he drove into the carpark and let Shelley direct him to her reserved bay. She got out of the car. The scene was so normal, yet her feelings were strange. A uniformed attendant came out of his hut, looking curiously at Sam.

' 'Morning, Miss Rushton. You've just missed Mr Dughall. He went out in the Mercedes.'

'Did he say where he was going?'

'Sorry, miss, he didn't.'

Shelley turned to Sam, clenching her fists tightly.

'He could be at a meeting. He could be having an early lunch. He might even have gone home for the day. There's no saying when he'll be back.'

Sam took her hand, unclenched the

fist and squeezed it gently. Sympathy and understanding flowed from him. Shelley felt stronger because he was by her side. They crossed the carpark to the building where the offices were and then she directed him into the lift that led up to the private suites. Sam turned his troubled brown gaze her way.

'I wish I had some idea of what we're looking for.'

Shelley found her words sticking on her lips. It wasn't only the legal caution that had prevented her voicing her suspicions to Heather, she still had to overcome her feelings of loyalty to her ex-fiancé. She'd almost decided to keep quiet, when the mental block suddenly dissolved, and she found herself confiding in Sam.

'I found delivery notes for cheap flour. We should be using top quality, and the customer research I did in the garage shows that people have been noticing the difference. Sales have been dropping for months.'

Sam asked tentatively, 'Did anyone at

Rushton's comment on the sales figures?'

Shelley felt better.

'Of course, but Brent's solution to the problem was for the company to take out massive loans and install new machinery.'

A soft chime announced their arrival. As the lift doors opened Shelley wondered what Sam was making of the old-fashioned oak offices. She felt pride and a fierce defensiveness. This was her family's company, and if Brent Dughall was stealing from it, she'd catch him and make him rue the day he ever lived. She was proud of Rushton's Bakery, and everyone who worked there. She smiled at the receptionist.

'Hello, Joyce. Is my father in?'

The perfectly-groomed lady with white hair smiled back.

'He's gone out for a long lunch, Miss Rushton, with those sales' reps from Japan, the ones who make the new machinery.'

Shelley felt the familiar sharp interest in all the business of the bakery.

'He got the loans, then?'

The receptionist grinned.

'Officially, I wouldn't know.'

'I hope you never retire, Joyce,' Shelley said, laughing, but knowing Joyce's discretion was part of her value. 'I'll get the details later, from my secretary, but first I need to visit the accounts section.'

She led Sam down an imposing, oak-panelled corridor. Sam seemed to be concentrating on the lush crimson carpet, but as they passed a door with Brent's name on a large brass plate, Sam lifted his head to look at her.

'Shouldn't we look in his office?'

'I'll find any discrepancies in the accounts,' Shelley murmured.

She wondered why she was whispering. She had every right to be where she was, and more than the right to check up on her suspicions. She pushed open the door to the accountants' offices. Several people looked up and smiled brightly. Shelley returned their greetings.

'Hello, yourselves. Is anyone doing work that can't be broken off? No? That's excellent. I'd like you all to take a long lunch, please. There isn't a problem, but I want to check up on a few matters, in private.'

Shelley waited until the last employee had filed out of the room before turning to Sam.

'I have to be careful. If we've made a mistake about this, it could ruin Brent's career.'

Sam shoved his hands deep in his pockets and wandered moodily around the office as Shelley sat herself at a computer terminal and started work. He was shamefully ignorant of computers and he knew it. He wished he knew more, then he might have been able to help her instead of wandering around the office like a spare part.

There was a photo of Shelley on one wall. She looked like a top model in her executive suit and she was shaking hands with Royalty as she accepted an award for excellence. Sam felt increasingly gloomy as he scanned the wall. Every picture he saw emphasised the gulf between his lifestyle and hers. Then he heard her soft gasp.

'I do not believe this.'

Sam walked across to where she was sitting at the computer. She still looked like his Shelley. She was wearing casual clothes, jeans, a purple sweater and soft boots, but the serious, businesslike expression on her face made her holiday clothes look out of place.

'Found something?' Sam asked.

Shelley's eyes met his. He could see the pain in them as she spoke.

'Brent's changed his passwords.'

'Then he's hiding something. Can you get into his files without passwords?'

She gave a short and bitter laugh.

'I set up the system! Brent only knows how to work it. I taught him how to set his passwords along with everything else. He obviously doesn't realise that I can override them any time I choose.'

She turned back to the computer and her fingers flew over the keyboard. Sam wanted to kill Brent Dughall for making Shelley miserable, causing her trouble. Sam watched Shelley while she ran her hands through her hair, muttered a soft curse and then furiously typed again. His heart ached with love for her, love and admiration. She was so clever and competent. She deserved all the luxury and success her skills brought her.

Columns of numbers raced across the screen so fast that Sam didn't even try to follow them. He could see that she'd got into the system and was manipulating data, comparing spreadsheets, turning figures into graphs. Brent Dughall might have fooled the accountants, but Sam had no doubt that Shelley would uncover the truth.

She sat back with a sigh, and then reached over for one final check. A printer next to the desk hummed into life. Shelley looked up at Sam with wide, hurt eyes. Her lips trembled.

'I still can't believe this.'

'Have you found a discrepancy?'

Her eyes narrowed and her voice turned vicious.

'Discrepancy! I'd call it wholesale theft!'

Sam knew her anger wasn't directed at him. He placed calming hands on her shoulders.

'Figures mean nothing to me. Tell me in plain English.'

Because the palms of his hands were flat on her shoulders, he could feel the faint, regular shivers that were racking her body. Her voice was full of strain.

'It's more than just flour. For more than a year, now, starting small and getting greedier with every passing week, Brent has been tampering with the accounts. He has been ordering cheap supplies, regular salt instead of sea salt, second-class salad, cheap shrimp bits instead of nice juicy prawns. No wonder our sales were dropping.'

Sam looked at the screen. There was a sick, uneasy feeling in his stomach. He had a premonition of danger.

'Could this information be wiped off the computer?'

Shelley shook her head.

'No, it's backed up every day and stored in the safe. I'm only printing out a paper copy to show my father.'

She turned her head away, and Sam heard sobs in her voice as she whispered her last few words.

'My father, and the police.'

★   ★   ★

Brent Dughall hated Joyce. The receptionist was always so self-possessed. She had no idea what it was like to struggle and strive the way he had to. She never looked busy, she never looked flustered, and she never lost the self-satisfied smirk that said she was so much better than he was. He hated her, but soon he'd be in the Caribbean, and he'd never have to hear her ladylike little voice again.

'Hello, Mr Dughall, you've just missed Miss Rushton. She and a visitor have gone to the accounts department.'

One of the young male accountants strolled past.

'Miss Rushton can visit us anytime. We've got an early lunch out of it.'

'She's sent you all away?' he asked and the young accountant nodded.

Brent had to stop himself striking out at the man. He clenched his fists and stalked past. His hands were shaking as he unlocked his office. He slammed the door behind him, but it didn't make him feel any better. He paced furiously around and around his desk while he thought. Occasionally, senior management asked the accounts staff to leave while they made a private check, but not often. If Shelley was in accounts with a visitor, he was in trouble, big trouble. It was time to cut and run.

Brent opened the top drawer of his desk and started to scoop out personal belongings. The phone on his desk rang, and his stomach churned while he looked at it. Should he answer? Beads of sweat formed on his top lip. He picked up the receiver with a hand that trembled.

'Hello?'

'Ah, Brent, lad, I'm glad I've caught you, very glad.'

Brent relaxed as he recognised the genial tones of Harry Rushton. Shelley's father sounded expansive and happy. Brent could hear the sounds of a restaurant in the background as he continued to speak.

'I thought you'd like to know that I've made a good deal on the price of the new machinery, a very good deal as it happens. Now, we don't usually do business of this magnitude in cash, but the Japanese insist, absolutely insist, so I'd like you to be at the handover as a witness. Can you meet me in my office, say in an hour's time?'

Brent felt his heart pounding. It was an effort to keep his voice steady.

'Would you like me to go to the bank

with you?' he asked and heard a fruity chuckle.

'No need, no need at all. The cash is waiting in the firm's safe.'

Brent put down the receiver and swept the last few personal items out of his desk and into his briefcase. It was crunch time, and he knew it. He could flee now, and live his whole life on a budget, or he could take one last desperate gamble and be happy for ever. Could he walk away, knowing that all that lovely money was in the firm's safe? Walk away when he'd been entrusted with the combination to that very safe?

He looked down at the open briefcase on his desk. There was a false bottom to that case and in the secret compartment was a weapon he'd acquired as private insurance, never imagining that he'd actually need to use it, but all that stood between him and his dream was Shelley — Shelley and her interfering visitor.

★ ★ ★

Sam's feelings of unease were mounting by the second.

'Shelley, I think we should call security.'

Shelley's gaze was on the sheets of paper whizzing out of the printer and her voice was absentminded as she replied, 'Let me finish this.'

Sam's hand reached for a telephone, but then stopped. This was Shelley's business. He should let her do it her way. But his jangling nerves wouldn't let him be silent.

'Have you forgotten the hit man?'

She smiled.

'I don't think he'd dare follow me into my own office.'

Sam's hand banged down on the desk.

'You don't know what Brent Dughall would dare. We have proof the man's been trying to kill you.'

Shelley's eyes flashed in annoyance.

'Don't be so macho. I can't go to

Daddy without facts. Give me two minutes.'

Sam exploded, and his hand immediately reached for the phone.

'I'm calling security now! We don't have two minutes to spare.'

'On the contrary,' a chilling voice broke in from the door. 'You'll have all eternity to spare, if you're not very careful.'

Sam's gaze went straight to the gun in Brent Dughall's hand, pointed directly at Shelley. Cold chills ran down Sam's back. He longed to see a security guard or Dwayne appear in the entrance, but there was only Brent Dughall, brandishing the gun that was menacing Shelley. It was up to Sam to save her. Brent gestured towards Shelley with the weapon.

'Open the safe,' he commanded.

She was staring at him with revulsion and disbelief.

'Brent, we were going to be married. I can't believe — '

His face twisted.

'Cut the girlie stuff and do as I say!'

Shelley simply stared at the man in frozen shock. Sam's gaze raked over his enemy, trying to assess the situation. It was impossible to tell what Brent Dughall normally looked like. Sam guessed he'd be quite handsome. But as Sam looked at the man's eyes, he saw that they were abnormally dilated and fixed in intensity. Brent Dughall was a man on the edge. Sam spoke very slowly and distinctly to Shelley, putting all the command and urgency that he could muster into his tone.

'Do as Brent says.'

Shelley's lovely face turned towards Sam. Her eyes were wide with shock, her cheeks as white as the snow-covered mountains. Her gaze searched Sam's face for a split second, then he saw her expression shift and he knew that she'd decided to obey Brent. She moved slowly towards the old-fashioned safe that stood in an alcove.

Sam watched Brent Dughall carefully. The man's muscles relaxed very slightly as he watched Shelley's fingers fluttering over the brass combination wheels of the lock, but he kept the gun trained unwaveringly at her heart. The door swung open and a large pile of banknotes could be seen on the top shelf. Sam wondered if Brent was used to dealing in real cash rather than numbers on a computer screen. He made his tone conversational.

'How are you going to carry all those banknotes?'

Brent looked up and around him, distracted for a moment.

'A bag maybe? Is there a bag?'

Sam seized his chance as Brent looked around. He was a doctor, not a warrior, but the Navy had taught him a lot, and he went straight for the gun in Dughall's right hand. Sam's hands closed around the man's wrist. He felt Dughall's muscles and tendons moving under his grip, and he knew the man was going to fire. All of his strength went into pulling the gun down and away from Shelley. He could smell the shot and felt the vibration before he heard it. He wasn't afraid. Part of him still couldn't believe that a real gun could be fired in an English office.

Then Brent swung around, trying to free his hand from Sam's grip, and as Sam's body followed the movement and he struggled for advantage, he saw the office chair next to Shelley. There was a black hole in the back with burn marks all around it. Rage towered inside Sam's heart. The maniac had tried to kill Shelley. A savage, furious, primitive instinct took over and Sam found himself fighting with a strength and skill that he hadn't known he possessed. It was soon over. Brent's knees buckled, and the man slid groggily to the carpet. Sam didn't dare let go of him. He shouted over his shoulder.

'Shelley, get rope, a belt, something.'

He heard a clattering and the light in the office grew brighter. Shelley appeared in his field of vision dragging an unwieldy Venetian blind. She snatched a pair of orange-handled scissors from the nearest desk and cut off a length of cord.

'More,' Sam panted, tying Brent's wrists as securely as he could. 'The man's a maniac. I don't want him to get loose.'

Shelley clipped more lengths of cord and helped Sam secure Brent's ankles. Then they stood up and looked at him. He made a fantastic sight. His grey suit was crumpled, his blond hair was tousled, but the man still looked like a regular businessman — until you looked at the cords that bound him.

Shelley picked up the telephone, and Sam heard her coolly and efficiently sending for assistance from the office security and the police. She also called her father. Then she came back and stood next to Sam. She looked at the bullet hole in the chair as if she couldn't believe it. He saw Shelley's lips tremble and he remembered the soft heart under the executive manner. Her smile wavered, but her voice was firm as she spoke.

'I guess I have to thank you for saving my life, again.'

Sam put his arm around her, intending to support her, but he felt her body tense. She wanted to stand on her own, and he couldn't blame her. This was no time to ask her to trust a man. Only a few seconds previously, the man she was technically engaged to had tried to blow off her head.

It pained him, but Sam knew that Shelley would have to deal with her emotions before she could find her way into his arms. He took his arm away from her shoulders. He could hear footsteps running along the corridor towards them. He looked urgently into Shelley's eyes.

'Will you be OK?'

Her chin tilted proudly.

'Of course.'

A distinguished, older man in a well-cut suit ran through the door.

Shelley threw herself into his arms. Sam watched them embrace for a long minute before he turned away feeling lonely. His work here was finished. Shelley didn't need him any more.

9

'Are you sure there's no-one else waiting?' Sam asked the nurse working alongside him in the hospital clinic.

She was reaching for her coat as she answered him.

'Get out of here, you slave driver! It's bad enough only having one weekend off in three, without you wanting to work late on a Friday!'

'Sorry,' Sam muttered, realising that it would be selfish to keep his staff any later. 'Today's clinic did seem to run on, but that emergency operation threw everything out of schedule. You get off and have a nice weekend. I'll finish up here.'

'It's all done,' his receptionist called from the doorway.

She, too, was wearing her coat and ready to leave.

Sam raised his voice and shouted

after his staff, 'Thank you! You're wonderful!'

But in secret he wished that he had a nice big pile of work to do. Work was the only thing that blunted the edge of his longing for Shelley. His mind was so well trained that, despite his heartbreak, each patient got his full attention, but the second work was over, the agony returned.

The last thing Sam wanted was a weekend off. He tidied a few items in the already immaculate room, and then gave up and walked slowly along the long, marble corridor that led to the car park. He had no idea how he was going to get through another weekend without Shelley. How long would it be before the pain subsided?

Three weeks had passed without a word, and he was beginning to accept that she'd never contact him, but far from learning to embrace that thought, it hurt him more every day. He thought about her every waking moment and her beautiful eyes haunted his dreams.

He couldn't stop remembering her kisses, her smile, her laughter. Even now, over the medical smells of the hospital, the smell of her perfume rose to haunt him. He closed his eyes and inwardly groaned.

'Indigestion, Doctor Gilday?' a silvery voice asked.

Sam looked wildly up and down the empty marble corridor until a low chuckle guided him to one of the large window embrasures. Perched on a stone windowsill, swinging her legs and looking stunning, was Shelley! Sam was knocked sideways by the reality, so much more alive and vital than his memories. He hunted urgently for a casual reaction, but ended up standing immobile, staring at her.

For one heart-stopping second, Shelley thought his immobile stance and frozen face signified rejection, but then his stunned disbelief melted into unmistakable joy. The way he said her name was a caress.

'Shelley?'

His tan was fading but he was still the doctor who had woken her that first moment in the cottage. He was wearing a white coat and stethoscope around his neck, but he looked exactly the same. Shelley placed a single kiss on his cheek and then drew back to examine every inch of him.

'How are you, Sam?'

His brown eyes were watching her as though he still couldn't believe she was truly standing in front of him.

'I'm fine. How are you?'

'Oh, fine,' Shelley answered lightly, but his intelligent gaze penetrated her very soul, and she knew that this man deserved the truth. 'Well, OK, you know?'

His eyes showed that he understood her very well.

'You've had a lot to work through.'

Shelley looked at the tips of her boots and said softly, 'I couldn't come any sooner.'

She felt his strong hands reaching out to touch hers.

'I'm just glad you're here now.'

She looked up and met his eyes. They were wide and soft and brown and blazing with love for her.

'I missed you,' she confessed.

'Have dinner with me?' Sam urged.

'I can't.'

He looked devastated.

'Can't or don't want to?'

Shelley hesitated on her next words, wondering if her request was too cheeky, but Sam was looking at her as if he would give her the moon if she asked for it, so she smiled at him and said, 'My Range Rover is ready to collect from the garage at Appleton. I was wondering, if you are free, if you might take me to collect it.'

She could see the exultation in his eyes. Sam ripped off his white coat and waved it around his head, grinning jubilantly.

'Let's go!'

With the snow now a memory, it took less than two hours to reach the Hawthornes' farm. Shelley glanced up into Sam's handsome face as they drove into the farmyard and she smiled at him. Conversation had been a bit sticky at first. She told him what little more she knew about Brent's embezzling, and they'd speculated as to what the outcome of the court case might be, but then they'd moved on to lighter subjects and they'd chatted easily as Sam's car, a comfortable saloon, glided along the open roads to Appleton.

Shelley's Range Rover, looking as good as new, stood in the Hawthornes' yard. As Shelley looked at it, she realised that she'd have to drive home alone rather than with Sam, and her heart sank. They'd discussed nothing of a personal nature, as yet. Mr Hawthorne appeared in his yard, smiling. He was dangling two sets of keys.

'Now then, you'll want to see the new kitchen in yonder cottage.'

It was impossible to refuse.

'Go on,' Mr Hawthorne urged, 'but mind you're back for eight. The young professor's coming for dinner, and so's

Dr Choudry, so don't be late.'

Number three Pippin Cottages was very, very cold. The Hawthornes had set the thermostat to one notch above freezing, to safeguard the plumbing, but they'd never dream of heating an empty cottage. The click of the door latch as it closed behind them and the sight of the sheepskin-covered couch brought back a flood of memories.

Shelley wrapped her arms around herself as if to hold in the tide of recollections as she followed Sam into the refurbished kitchen. There was no trace left of the fire.

Shelley looked at Sam.

'Do you remember — '

But he'd started to say the same words at the same moment.

They looked at each other and laughed. Shelley felt close enough to him to admit, 'I've thought of you, Sam. I tried at first to block the memories, but it didn't work.'

Sam spoke very gently.

'You've been in my heart and in my

mind from the second I met you.'

His chocolate-brown gaze locked on to hers with an intensity there was no escaping.

'I've missed this place.'

Shelley didn't want to escape this moment.

'I've missed you,' he said and the smile that he gave her came straight from his heart.

Shelley wanted to lose herself in his love. He reached for her face and cradled it in his hands. His lips touched hers, and Shelley sensed love and commitment.

Her whole body came alive. She moved away slightly so that she could watch his face.

'I've missed us,' she told him softly.

She rested her head against his solid chest. He wrapped his arms around her and rubbed the top of her head with his chin.

'Have you forgiven me for the lies that brought us together?'

Shelley lifted her head and looked

directly into his eyes.

'It's all forgotten.'

'I so wanted you to trust me.'

Shelley smiled as she remembered.

'And I wanted to trust my feelings for you.'

Sam kissed her and then breathed deeply and drew back.

'There's so much to talk about. Do you think you could be happy with a hard-working doctor?'

Shelley nodded, but she saw his eyes cloud over with doubt.

'One of the reasons I didn't contact you was because there are so many problems between our lifestyles. Your house is thirty miles from the hospital for instance.'

Shelley smiled as she imagined Sam measuring the distance. She couldn't resist teasing him a little.

'Are you so keen to live with my father?'

Sam looked very surprised, and then he grinned broadly.

'Oh! It never occurred to me. You

mean we should get a new place?'

'It's usual,' Shelley told him with a chuckle in her voice. 'You can measure the road again and find a point halfway between the bakery and the hospital.'

Sam swept her up in a crushing bear hug.

'With a smart cookie like you, how can our marriage go wrong?'

'It might never get off the ground if you don't propose to me,' Shelley pointed out cheekily.

Sam's eyes held all the love in the world.

'Shelley, darling, Shelley, will you do me the honour of becoming my wife?'

Her heart softened and she allowed Sam to tuck her up into his warm embrace and hug her and kiss her until she melted in his arms.

'That's settled, then,' he said happily, some time later. 'We'll be married as soon as possible. Would you like to honeymoon at this cottage?'

Shelley looked around at the country

cottage where it all started. Then she shivered in the cold, February air of England and wrapped her arms more tightly around Sam.

'How would you feel about somewhere tropical?'

Sam looked a little disappointed, but he said, 'Anywhere you like.'

Shelley remembered Sam telling her how unhappy he'd been in Africa, and she was touched by his willingness to travel for her sake.

'We'll stay here if you like, but how about Hawaii?'

His expression lightened.

'Ah, now you're talking! Warm, gorgeous and civilised.'

'And for our second, third, fourth and hundredth honeymoons, Doctor Gilday,' Shelley said, wrapping her arms around his neck and kissing him again, 'I'll buy you this cottage as a summer retreat.'

'We can't afford — ' Sam began.

Then he caught himself and looked down at Shelley smiling.

'I think I'm going to like having a rich wife.'

She laughed up at him happily.

'You're going to love it,' she promised. 'I'll make sure of that.'

THE END

We do hope that you have enjoyed reading this large print book.

Did you know that all of our titles are available for purchase?

We publish a wide range of high quality large print books including:
Romances, Mysteries, Classics
General Fiction
Non Fiction and Westerns

Special interest titles available in large print are:
The Little Oxford Dictionary
Music Book, Song Book
Hymn Book, Service Book

Also available from us courtesy of Oxford University Press:
Young Readers' Dictionary
(large print edition)
Young Readers' Thesaurus
(large print edition)

For further information or a free brochure, please contact us at:
Ulverscroft Large Print Books Ltd.,
The Green, Bradgate Road, Anstey,
Leicester, LE7 7FU, England.
Tel: (00 44) **0116 236 4325**
Fax: (00 44) **0116 234 0205**

Other titles in the
Linford Romance Library:

THREE TALL TAMARISKS

Christine Briscomb

Joanna Baxter flies from Sydney to run her parents' small farm in the Adelaide Hills while they recover from a road accident. But after crossing swords with Riley Kemp, life is anything but uneventful. Gradually she discovers that Riley's passionate nature and quirky sense of humour are capturing her emotions, but a magical day spent with him on the coast comes to an abrupt end when the elegant Greta intervenes. Did Riley love Greta after all?

SUMMER IN HANOVER SQUARE

Charlotte Grey

The impoverished Margaret Lambart is suddenly flung into all the glitter of the Season in Regency London. Suspected by her godmother's nephew, the influential Marquis St. George, of being merely a common adventuress, she has, nevertheless, a brilliant success, and attracts the attentions of the young Duke of Oxford. However, when the Marquis discovers that Margaret is far from wanting a husband he finds he has to revise his estimate of her true worth.

CONFLICT OF HEARTS

Gillian Kaye

Somerset, at the end of World War I: Daniel Holley, unhappily married to an ailing wife and father of four grown-up children, is attracted to beautiful schoolteacher Harriet Bray, but he knows his love is hopeless. Daniel's only daughter, Amy, who dreams of becoming a milliner and is caught up in her love for young bank clerk John Tottle, looks on as the drama of Daniel and Harriet's fate and happiness gradually unfolds.